TRAPPED

IN

LOVE

ERNEST
MORRIS

GOOD 2 GO PUBLISHING

TRAPPED IN LOVE
Written by Ernest Morris
Cover Design: Davida Baldwin - Odd Ball Designs
Typesetter: Mychea
ISBN: 978-1-947340-50-3
Copyright © 2019 Good2Go Publishing
Published 2019 by Good2Go Publishing
7311 W. Glass Lane • Laveen, AZ 85339
www.good2gopublishing.com
https://twitter.com/good2gobooks
G2G@good2gopublishing.com
www.facebook.com/good2gopublishing
www.instagram.com/good2gopublishing

CHAPTER ONE

"Mom, that's not fair. All my friends are going to be there. I'll only be gone for an hour."

"Well you're not them, Karma. What you should be worrying about is getting your home-work done for school Monday, not some damn party."

Karma was the youngest of three siblings and couldn't have fun like the other girls on her block. Her two older twin sisters, Rynesha and Dynesha, on the other hand, got to do and go as they pleased. Their mother never complained about them coming in the house late, because they were considered adults. Karma envied her sisters, and they both knew it. They were beautiful, but Karma, by far, had the best figure of the three. There were plenty of times that guys came over to see them but couldn't keep their eyes off of Karma. She enjoyed the atten-tion, knowing that they wanted her more than they wanted her sisters.

At the age of seventeen, Karma had blossomed from a shy skinny little girl, into a beautiful, voluptuous, petite young woman. Standing at five foot three, she was half Puerto Rican and black, with long black silky hair that came down to her lower back. She looked like a younger version of Eva Mendez. All the boys at school had the hots for her, but her eyes were set on one particular guy. Me! We were in the same gym class at Scranton High. The only problem was, I had a girlfriend.

"It's the weekend, we don't have homework."

"Well you can study or something. Until you bring that D up in math, you won't be going anywhere. This is your last year of school before you're off to college. You can't afford to be messing up now. If your friends want to come over here and study with you, they can, but you're not going out."

"But, Mom . . ."

"Don't you 'but Mommy' me. This conversation is over for now. We'll discuss this tomorrow when I get home from work. I'll call and check up on you later," her mother replied, heading out the door.

Karma peeked out the window until her mother pulled off, then ran upstairs to change clothes. Despite what her mother was talking about, she was heading to that party. As long as she was back before 7:00 a.m., she would be just fine. After calling her friends and telling them to pick her up, she quickly got dressed, then fixed her hair and makeup.

Forty-five minutes later they were pulling up at Levels night club on the south side. You could see from the outside that the place was packed with mostly college students getting their groove on, or drinking. Security was at the front door scanning IDs and searching people as they entered. Karma and her two girlfriends stood in the long line waiting to get in. It seemed like they were going to be standing outside forever, when I tapped her on the shoulder. She turned around to see who touched her.

"What's up, shorty? What y'all doing standing in this long-ass line?" I asked with a smirk.

"Same as you, trying to get in," her friend Genesis cut in, looking sassy with her hands on her hip.

My first thought was to tell her to mind her business because I thought she was trying to be smart. But her facial expression said she was only fucking around. I turned to my boys who came with me, giving them a head nod, and they started walking toward the entrance.

"Y'all coming or what?"

Karma looked at her friends and they all hunched their shoulders as if to say hell yeah, then followed us inside. Because I knew the bouncer at the door, we only had to pay half price. We still hooked him up with a generous tip, though, because I was strapped, and so were my boys. Once inside, me and my boys went over to the bar to get a drink, while Karma and her girls went on the dance floor. I found myself checking her out from a distance, but that stopped once my girl walked in.

"I thought you were going to meet me at the after hour?" Abby asked, wrapping her arms around me.

"I'm still going afterward."

I greeted her with a quick kiss, tasting her watermelon lip gloss. She was rocking a tight fitted one-piece dress, with stilettos. Her beauty alone demanded so much attention when she stepped into a room. When I palmed her ass, she slapped my hand away.

"Stop that!" she said, looking around to see if someone was watching.

Everyone in school knew that Abby and I

were an item, but she never liked to show it in public. That was one of our problems, amongst other things, but I still loved her. She wasn't one for public affection, and I was. I liked showing off my chick to all the haters. It didn't bother me too much, though, because most of my time was spent in the streets getting at a dollar. I guess you can say that I was living a double life. An A student by day, and a hustler by night.

"What do you want to drink?" I asked, waving a twenty-dollar bill in the air for one of the bartenders. She made her way over toward us.

"My regular, baby," Abby replied.

After ordering her drink, Abby gave me another kiss, then stepped off to go dance with her friends, while we stayed at the bar drinking. To the naked eye, it would have seemed like I was drinking with them, but I was only drinking cranberry and orange juice. I was too young to drink, but that didn't stop my boys from doing it. I could see Abby through the crowd dancing with some dude. It didn't bother me one bit. Besides, that's what we come to clubs for, isn't it? An hour later, she came back over and whispered in my ear.

"I'm ready to go somewhere and fuck. Let's

get out of here."

She reached down and rubbed my dick through my jeans, licked her lips, then sashayed away toward the exit. You already know, that was my cue to bounce.

"Fellas, I'm out. I will get at you niggas in the morning."

"Don't forget we have to meet up with Jazz in the morning to pick up the new shipment," Champ said, giving me a pound.

"I know," I yelled, following behind Abby.

As soon as we were both inside my truck, shit heated up real quick. Abby got on her knees in the passenger seat, unfastened my pants, and pulled my dick out. I pulled out of the park-ing spot around the corner from the club and headed up toward my crib on Webster Ave. We didn't even make it, before her head was boun-cing up and down in my lap. I had to admit, my girl's head game was on point, but it never could get me off. I had to be in the pussy before I could bust.

"Damn, you gonna make me crash," I moaned, trying to keep my eyes on the road.

"Pull over then."

"Hold on," I replied, trying to hurry home.

I pulled into my driveway and put the truck in park. Before I could do anything else, Abby had her dress raised to her waist and was climbing on top of me in the driver's seat. My truck was bombed out, so I wasn't worried about anyone walking past and catching us. It was dark as hell outside anyway. She pulled her panties to the side and slowly lowered her body down, guiding my dick into her already wet pussy. It felt so good that I damn near became a minute man.

"Yessss, Daddy, oh shiiittt, it feels so good," Abby whispered in my ear as I gripped her ass and guided her up and down on my shaft.

Minutes later, I was shooting my load deep into her. Abby kept working her vaginal muscles around my dick, until she released her own fluids. She reached into the glove compartment for some tissue to wipe off with, then fixed her dress. Once we both finished, we headed inside to finish what she started.

~ ~ ~

The next morning, I went to meet up with Jazz to pick up some more work. I was supposed to pick up Stizz and Champ, but neither answered their phones. I figured they were both somewhere laid up with one of the many females that were at the club last night. Whatever the reason, they still should have been ready to roll out with me.

"Fuck it! Looks like I'm rolling by myself this time," I mumbled, pulling into the Gerrity's parking lot on Moosic Ave. It was only down the street from my crib, so it didn't take long once I got the call.

As I sat in my truck waiting for Jazz, my cellphone started vibrating. I pulled it out of my pocket and looked at the screen. It was Champ. At the same time, Jazz pulled up beside me. I sent Champ to voicemail and got out of my vehicle.

"What's up with you?" Jazz asked, holding his hand out. I leaned down, looked at the bad chick he had in the passenger seat, and then shook his hand.

"Ain't shit. Trying to hurry up and catch up with my crew. You got that for me, bro?"

My attention at the moment was on the female. She had on a pair of white tights and a Polo jacket. Her legs were cocked open, with his hand between them. When Jazz moved his hand to reach in the backseat, I could see the wet spot coming from where he was playing with her pussy. It had soaked through the fabric of her tights. She noticed I was staring and gave me an enticing smile. She may have been riding with him, but I could tell he wasn't the only one fucking her. I shook my head and focused back on the matter at hand.

"Here you go." He passed me the shopping bag with the work in it. "You have the money now? Or should I grab it from you later when we meet up?"

"Naw, that's not necessary, I have the whole thing for you right now."

I went back to my truck and grabbed the gym bag with the money for the two keys he had just given me. He already knew how I like doing business. That's why there was never a problem between us when it came down to making transactions. I could easily get whatever I wanted from him on consignment, but I liked money on the wood.

"That's why I fucks with you, Jordan, because you know how to conduct business. You need to show that lil nigga Champ the ropes before he fucks over the wrong nigga."

"Watch your mouth."

He wanted to keep talking shit about my friend, but quickly changed the subject when he noticed the look on my face.

"I got some new shit coming in from Miami next week. It's even better than what we have now. When that shit hits the streets, motherfuckers gonna be stumbling over each other to get their hands on it. I'll let you know when it comes in."

"Sounds good to me. Get at me."

I gave him a fist bump, then got back in my truck. As they pulled off, the shorty in the passenger seat stuck her tongue out and started twirling it around her lips. I put my middle finger up at her and she mouthed the word "When?" then rolled the window up before I could respond. Once back in the truck, I called Champ back.

"Nigga, shit could have went south just now because y'all wasn't with me," I snapped soon as he answered.

"Stop bitching. These motherfuckers already know what it is out here. Fuck with us and end up in a river somewhere stinking. We good on the product?"

"Yeah we good. Where you at right now?"

"At the telly."

"Which one, nigga, so I can drop this work off to you and Stizz."

"We're at the Red Carpet Inn."

"Bring us some McDonald's, too, while you at it. We hungry as fuck, bro," Stizz yelled out in the background.

I ended the call and then stopped at the McDonald's over on Southside. After grabbing their food, I headed over to the Red Carpet Inn. Champ came to the door when he saw me pull up. Out of nowhere, two niggas in black hoodies jumped out of a gray Ford Taurus and tried to sneak up on him. I hopped out with my Glock .40 in hand.

"Get down," I yelled, at the same time letting off four rounds in the direction of the gunmen.

Champ got low and ducked back into the hotel. The gunmen tried to turn and aim in my direction, but I was too quick for them. I was able to hit the first one with a wig shot, but the other one ducked behind a car. I couldn't see where he was hiding.

"Boom!"

The sound of the cannon was deafening. I peeked up from the car, to see Champ standing over the other body. He was holding his .357 in his right hand. Stizz also stood by the door with his hand clutched around his gun. He kept looking inside the room.

"You good, nigga?"

"I'm straight," I replied, walking toward them. "Who the fuck was these niggas?"

"I'm quite sure they know," Stizz said, pointing to the two bitches sitting on the bed scared to death.

All along, they were trying to set us up to get robbed, and the shit backfired on them. I gave Champ a look, and he already knew what it meant. He walked over to the girls and put a bullet through both of their heads. We rushed to our cars, and got the fuck out of Dodge before the pigs arrived. Lucky for us the only people that saw us were just as dirty as we were. They used the hotel for drug activities and tricking. The desk clerk had dialed 911 when she heard the gunshots. She never saw us, though, so we were in the clear, or so we thought.

~ ~ ~

A week later, I was at the Steamtown Mall, when two plainclothes officers pulled me over as

I was leaving the garage. I knew they had nothing on me, so I wasn't worried. That was until they searched my truck and pulled out the dope I had stashed in my secret box. I wondered how the hell they knew about that. They snatched me up and took me back to the station for questioning.

I was held in prison until my trial. It didn't take long for the jury to convict me. Lackawanna County had been known for railroading people, but never did I imagine this. Due to the amount of dope and the fact that the judge hated drug dealers, I was sentenced to seven and a half to fifteen years in a state institution. My lawyer told me to be patient and said that she would be appealing it. Abby watched from the back of the courtroom in tears as they escorted me out in shackles.

CHAPTER TWO

I spent about two months at SCI-Phoenix, before being transferred to SCI-Camphill. Abby came to visit me every other week, and I either talked to her on the phone or used the kiosk to message her during the day. She sent me mad freak photos of herself to help occupy my time when I was alone in my cell. Once they had that big statewide lockdown over some COs getting sick, she stopped sending them because I wasn't getting the original copies anymore. My cellmate was some dude from Harrisburg. He was doing life in prison for killing his girlfriend and the dude she was creeping with. Me and him became friends due to our mutual friends.

"Yo, they about to call us for commissary," Reek said, putting on his blue uniform.

"I'm ready," I told him while sitting at the desk writing a letter to my girl. "I'm trying to get one of those kitchen workers to bring back some extra chicken tonight so I can throw some in my soup."

"You're probably the only one in prison that don't like cooking," he joked. "All you want to do is eat plain soups with crackers."

"Don't hate me, nigga."

"Seriously, what's up with shorty in medical? She been checking you out since you been here," Reek told me as he sat on his bunk.

"She alright, but she keep playing games. I only played with the pussy two times. She keep talking about not yet. I don't have time for the bullshit. Either you with it or you not."

"I feel you," Reek said as the door popped open for commissary. "We out, bro."

We headed out the cell to get in line with the other inmates. As we made our way to the beginning of the block, I was stopped by an officer.

"Mr. Smith, you have to go over to medical."

"Can I go when I get back?"

"No, go now. I will make sure you get down there when you come back. Here is your pass." As mad as I was at that moment, I did what I was told.

The infirmary was empty except for the inmate workers and a couple of other staff members. The guard was sitting at his desk reading a newspaper when I arrived. He looked up, grabbed my pass, and then told me to have a seat until called. I sat there for about twenty minutes before the nurse called me into the examination room.

"Take your shirt off and have a seat on the table, Mr. Smith," she said, typing on the computer. Once she was finished, she walked to the door and yelled out to the officer: "I'm going to be taking some X-rays, so this door will be closed for a while."

"Okay," the officer looked up and replied, then kept on reading his paper.

Usually there had to be two people present when dealing with an inmate, but there was only one. The nurse closed the door, then turned to me with a smile on her face. I wasn't expecting this, so it kind of caught me off guard.

"I told you to be patient and it would pay off. Now here's your chance to show me that I made a mistake by making you wait so long. We only have ten minutes, so make the best of it."

She pulled down her scrubs and got onto the table I was sitting on. All objections went out the door once I saw how beautiful her pussy was. My dick instantly swelled up, trying to break through my pants. The nurse helped me pulled them down to my ankles, then positioned herself on top of me. She lowered her body onto my girth with ease. I slid right in without even thinking about protection. That decision would probably come back and haunt me later. Right now, I didn't care.

"Mmmmmm, fuck yeah! This is just what the fuck I needed," I mumbled. I wasn't even worried about getting my canteen anymore. Getting my dick wet, even if it was only going to be once, was better than what I would have been doing in my cell.

"Damn, I'm so wet," the nurse said, sticking a finger inside her pussy the same time as my dick moved in and out of her. "You gonna make this pussy cum?"

"You better do it now, cause I'm about to," I told her, feeling my balls tightening up from each stroke.

She had her eyes closed, biting down on her bottom lip. As much as I tried to stall, it wasn't working. I closed my eyes and flexed my hips to meet hers.

"You feel so good," I murmured. "That's right, baby, take all of it."

She did exactly that, bouncing up and down on my dick like a cowgirl riding a horse. She continued to move her body, countering my movements in perfect rhythm. Placing her hands on my chest, I felt her body start to convulse, letting me know that she was on the brink of cumming. I squeezed her ass cheeks apart and stuck a finger in her hole. The sensation of both my finger and dick penetrating her most sensitive holes, sent her over the edge, releasing a powerful orgasm. It poured from her body like a fountain. Seeing the look on her face caused me to cum abruptly. She collapsed on top of me.

"Shit, you almost made me scream, boy," she whispered, getting off the medical table and putting her pants back on. I did the same.

"Damn, that was good."

After our clothes were fixed, she walked over to the door and opened it. The guard was just coming down to check on us. A couple minutes later, we would have been caught red-handed. He looked at her, then me, and continued down the corridor doing his security check.

"That was close." She smiled. "Next time we have to pick a better spot, and I know just the place."

"Oh, so there's going to be a next time, huh?"

I squeezed her soft ass as I headed toward the door.

"Don't play yourself, there better be."

I retrieved my pass from the officer's desk and headed back to my block without answering her. Lucky for me, the last few stragglers were heading down to get their commissary, so I grabbed my bag and got in line with them.

~ ~ ~

"What's up, baby?"

"Nothing, doing my hair before I go to the doctor's."

"Damn, this is the third time in two months that you had to go see a doctor. What's wrong with you?" I asked, getting a bit suspicious.

Lately Abby had been distancing herself from me and I didn't know why. Ever since I was transferred to SCI-Waymart, the visits slowed down drastically. They went from once a week, to once a month, and she was only fifteen minutes away. She would always make up some lame excuse about work or her mother being sick.

Just the other day, one of the niggas that was always in the visiting room with me, told me that his girl had seen Abby at the mall hugged up with the next nigga. At first I didn't believe him, but then he put me on the phone with her. She said that she remembered us because of how beautiful we looked together, and then ran down all the details of what she saw, even telling me that she looked pregnant. After giving Yayah the phone back, I called Abby to confront her about what I just heard.

"I told you my mom has been sick the last few months. She had me going to the appointments with her because she couldn't drive herself."

It took everything in my power not to snap, but her lies were starting to take a toll on me. Tired of hearing the bullshit, I decided to put it all on the forefront.

"Listen, I know your mom's not sick. Who is this nigga you been fucking with?"

"What are you talking about? I haven't been with anyone since—"

"Bitch, don't lie to me," I snapped, cutting her off. "You haven't been up here in months, and you expect me to believe that you're not fucking some other nigga?"

Silence!

"Jordan, I was lonely out here," Abby stated, finally breaking down. "You weren't here to take care of me."

"Who is the nigga you creeping around with?" Silence again! "You know what, fuck you and him. I hope he's sucking that pussy right."

"Baby, it's not like that. Let me ex—" I hung up on her.

There was nothing more for us to talk about. She had chosen what side she wanted to be on. I had to do this time without worrying about what nigga was digging my girl's back out. Besides, I needed to focus on my appeal. It had already been denied twice, so this was my last chance at it. My lawyer had stopped filing motions for me a long time ago because I ran out of money to pay him. Somehow, all the money I had stashed while selling drugs, miraculously disappeared.

Shit was definitely falling apart for me. That appeal was the only thing I had to look forward to. I headed back over to my cube to study my transcripts some more until they called for count. I was going to find a way out of this shit, one way or the other.

Chapter Three

Karma sat on the bed painting her toenails and watching *Paradise Hotel* on Hulu, the reality show about people trying to find love through the process of elimination. She shook her head at how gullible some people could be when it came to the opposite sex. Her two sisters came bursting into the room wearing only panties and bras.

"Let us borrow those two dresses you bought last month," Rynesha said, heading straight for the closet.

"For what?" Karma replied, pressing pause on her 72-inch flat-screen television that was mounted to the wall.

"What else, bitch? We have dates," Dynesha chimed in. She watched as her twin sister lay both dresses on the bed next to Karma. "I want the red one."

"Don't mess my shit up," Karma said as they slipped into the dresses.

Dynesha rolled her eyes and walked out of the room, followed by Rynesha. Karma shook her head then continued watching her show. Unlike her sisters, she had a good job as a paralegal and was studying to be a lawyer. Dynesha and Rynesha loved the streets to much to even consider working anywhere. Their money came from messing around with big-time hustlers. They would spend crazy bread on them and lace them with designer labels and expensive gifts, all for a piece of pussy at the end of the night. Sex was like an addiction to her sisters, but not for her.

Karma had a boyfriend, but he wasn't living up to her expectations. Sex only lasted two minutes, and his head game was next to nonexistent. He loved getting it, but wouldn't reciprocate the favor, and when he did, she never reached an orgasm. She couldn't even muster up a reason for staying with him.

The truth was, ever since that night at Levels night club, she couldn't stop thinking about Jordan. She had heard through the neighborhood of his arrest and wanted to reach out to him, but didn't want to interfere in his relationship.

"When Mommy comes home, tell her I put the rent money in her dresser," Dynesha said, peeking back in the room. "If we're not coming home tonight, I'll text you."

"Whatever! Y'all tricks know y'all not coming home tonight," Karma joked, sucking her teeth.

Dynesha smiled and headed downstairs to catch up with Rynesha. Left in the house alone, Karma decided to take a quick shower, then get back to watching her show. She stripped down to only her panties, then headed in the bathroom.

"Damn, I look good," she said, checking herself in the mirror.

After taking a shower and then putting on a pair of boy shorts and a wifebeater, Karma went downstairs to grab her Chinese food she had in the microwave. Just as she was heading back up the stairs, her mom walked in the door with some man she had never seen before. He looked like an exact replica of Jordan, but the older version. She wondered if it was his dad, or some other relation. Her thoughts were interrupted by the sound of her mother's voice.

"I thought you were sleep. Where are your sisters?"

"Out as usual. Dynesha left the money for you though."

"This is my friend James. James, this is my youngest daughter, Karma. I would have introduced you to the twins, but their hot asses is out running the streets with God knows who," her mother said playfully.

"Nice to meet you, Karma," James said in a deep, baritone voice.

Karma greeted her mother's friend, noticing that his eyes were glued on what she was wearing. She felt naked and continued up the steps. He watched her ass jiggle with each step she took until she was out of his view. When she sat on her bed, her mind went back to Jordan. She decided she would write him a letter tomorrow at work.

~ ~ ~

It was 2:30 a.m. when Karma was awakened by loud moaning coming from downstairs. She hopped out of bed and headed in that direction.

"Mmmmmm! Oh shit! That's right, suck it."

As Karma made her way down the steps, the moaning got louder. She could see two figures near the couch, engaged in a sexual act. She thought that her sisters had brought some random niggas back to the house again instead of going to a hotel. She had to warn them about their mother having company also. As soon as she reached the bottom of the steps, she could see who the figures were. Her left hand quickly went over her mouth. Karma's mother was down on her knees between the man legs, giving him a blowjob. He had his head leaned back against the cushion of the couch.

Slurp, slurp, slurp was the only sound you could hear besides more moaning.

Instead of her going back up the stairs, Karma stood there watching. This wasn't the first time she had seen her mother sexing a man. She and her sisters use to peek through the keyhole when they were younger. Dynesha and Rynesha learned a lot from watching their mother, so did Karma in her own way. She continued watching until he looked over at her. She tried to run away, but her feet wouldn't move. He gave her a smile, then grabbed her mother's head and began pushing it up and down, the whole time never taking his eyes off of Karma.

What he did next took her by total surprise. He pulled her up on to his lap, positioning her pussy in line with his rock-hard dick. Before inserting it in her wet hole, he started jerking it up and down with his right hand so Karma could see it's full length. Her panties quickly got soaked at the sight of it. It had to be the biggest dick she'd ever seen. He stroked it a few more times before inserting it deep inside her mom's love tunnel.

"Yeesssss, daddy," she heard her mother moan.

Karma could see him still watching her as he bounced her mother up and down on his shaft. One of her hands subconsciously made its way between the waistline of her shorts, down to her own wetness. She stuck two fingers inside her hole.

"Ssssssssss," Karma hissed, knowing her fingers weren't doing their job. What she really could use right now was a hard dick.

She sat down on the bottom step and continued fingering herself. It felt so good that she got lost in her own thoughts. She couldn't believe what she was doing in front of a complete stranger and enjoying it. He picked her mom up and flipped her over on the couch. Placing her legs on his shoulders, he entered her missionary style. The more her mother screamed, the deeper he went until he pulled out, squirting all over her stomach. He looked over to see if Karma was still enjoying the show, but she was gone.

She had made it back to her room, taken off her shorts, and was lying in her bed trying to finish what she started. This wasn't her usual get one off performance though. This was that, "I'm really horny and need to get fucked hard and fast performance." With her eyes closed, Karma stuck her vibrator deeper inside and turned it on high, trying to enjoy the feeling it was giving her. She imagined that it was Jordan delivering the beat down and started rotating her hips a little faster.

"Looks like you could use some help with that," a voice said, startling her.

Karma eye's immediately opened in shock and nervousness. Standing in the doorway was the man that was just downstairs having sex with her mother. He stared directly at the vibrator that was hanging halfway out of her vagina. She didn't know if she should scream, or run. He looked around the hallway, then stepped into the room, closing the door behind him.

"Get out my room before I scream," Karma said, pulling the blanket over her exposed body.

"Chill out! I thought you liked what you saw downstairs. It's not that deep, ma," he said, opening the door. "If you change your mind, you know where to find me."

Soon as he left, Karma jumped to her feet and locked the door. She took a deep breath then sat back on her bed, staring into space.

Chapter Four

Time started flying after the first couple of years here. Me and some chick name Ms. Thomas had been rendezvousing in different locations of the prison every week, getting our freak on. Yeah, I guess you can say my fun didn't stop just because I was transferred to a new prison. It actually worked in my favor. Ms. Thomas, who was on the nursing staff, lived a couple of blocks from me in Scranton. I always knew she had a crush on me, but never acted on it. When she saw me walking through the halls one day, she pulled me to the side and told me that I was going to enjoy being here with her as long as I could keep a secret. Oh course I needed to know what that secret was. She smiled at me, then grabbed my dick. A couple of days later, our sexcapade started.

There were two other inmates I became cool with that knew about our arrangement because they also had one of their own with two other nurses. They chose us, we didn't chose them, and everyone kept their mouths shut. It was the code of the prison. Break that code and be dealt with by your own peers. Life was looking good for me, being in this fucked-up situation.

One day that all changed when the security captain called me to his office. From the look on his face, I knew this wasn't a social visit. I sat in the chair across from his desk with my hands resting on my lap.

"There has been some disturbing news floating around this prison about you and a couple other inmates," he began, leaning forward on the desk. "I'm only going to ask you one time, so don't lie to me."

"Okay, ask away," I replied, giving him my full attention.

"Which nurse has been propositioning you for sexual favors, and what has she been giving you in return?"

"Huh! Nobody," I lied, quickly trying to shut the conversation down. "I go over to work then come back to my block. You sure you have the right person?"

"I'm positive, and unless you want to be placed in the RHU, under investigation until we find out what's going on, you need to start talking," Captain Pronoski stated. "We have been watching Sarah Thomas for quite some time, and we're well aware of her extracurricular activities in this facility with other inmates. I can guarantee if you talk now, there will be no repercussions toward you. However, if you don't talk to me and we find out you were involved, we will be charging you and everyone else."

"Like I said before, sir, I don't know what you're talking about. I had nothing to do with Ms. Thomas besides helping her move the patients in the infirmary when asked."

After grilling me for another hour, he let me go back to my block. I knew he didn't have anything on me when he threatened to charge me. You can't charge an inmate with a crime unless one was committed, and our sexual encounters were consensual. I didn't assault or force myself upon her. The only thing they could do is write me up for having relations with a staff member, and send me to the hole or transfer me. She could be arrested, though, for abuse of power. Just in case, when I got back to the block, I called home to let my cousin know what was going on. I needed my family to know what happened in case something popped off.

~ ~ ~

Rumors had started circulating throughout the prison that I had been talking to security, causing people to look at me differently. What they didn't know was, I didn't tell them shit. That's why they had been constantly harassing me. I was in the bathroom washing clothes when everything went black. Whatever had been thrown over my head was being held close to my neck, causing me to lose oxygen. My body was knocked down to the floor, and I was covered with kicks and stomps. I couldn't snatch off what was covering my face, because the kicks were landing there too.

"So you wanna be a snitch motherfucker, huh?" The voice was coming from someone kicking me on my right side. I could hear the heavy breathing between his words. I was surprised that our block officer didn't hear all the commotion.

"Yeah he do. He's a bitch," another voice whispered, this time on my left.

I couldn't talk to defend myself verbally, and there were too many of them for me to try to defend myself physically. The beatings, accusations, and insults kept coming until the computer in my head crashed and shut down. I woke up a week later in the Geisinger Hospital Unit, recovering from multiple grand mal seizures, followed by a medically induced coma.

A few days after I woke up, I stopped seizing and was showing signs of being able to move around on my own. That was all those bitches were waiting on so they could send me to the infirmary. I was told I'd be in there for a few weeks while my broken ribs and nose healed up. Then I would be transferred back to general population, so the ass whippings could continue. I wasn't going out like that though. Someone would surely be going out with me the next time. They had moved the officer off the block because he wasn't doing his job. He was too busy setting up a date with another officer after work, instead of paying more attention to what was happening on the block.

It seemed like my world was suddenly starting to fall apart. Ms. Thomas was given the option of resigning or being fired. Oh course she took the first option. I never heard from her again. They placed me on C1 for a week, before moving me back to M1. I never found out who had jumped me in the bathroom. I guess whoever did it realized I wasn't a snitch, because no one tried anything else. I was sitting in the dayroom watching *Equalizer 2*, when I heard the CO call my name.

"You called me?" I asked, approaching the desk.

"Yeah, you have a visit. Hurry up before they stop movement," she said, writing out a pass.

I was dressed and heading over to the visiting room in record time, anxious to see who came to visit me. For some strange reason, I was hoping that it was Abby waiting for me. That thought was erased from my head when I stepped onto the dance floor. It was my cousin Lil D. He had come to see how I was doing. Somehow he had found out who jumped me, and sent word to a couple of his friends here at the prison. They made everyone involved check into protective custody. The threat was neutralized for now.

We talked for hours about what was going on in the streets. He wanted me to come back to Philly when I got out, but I needed to think about that. Anyway, I had too much time left to even think about where I would be going when I was released.

"I'll come back up here to check on you in a couple of weeks," Lil D said, getting up to leave. "My shorty out there's probably getting impatient. Bye, you bitch-ass nigga." He laughed. I didn't!

"Watch your mouth, cousin. I'm not that dude anymore," I said, giving him a serious stare.

I wasn't going to allow him, or anybody, for that matter, to call me anything other than my real fucking name. Respect went both ways, like confused sexuality, and niggas were sleeping on me if they thought I was comfortable with the confusion. I knew it was sort of my fault for not checking niggas from the door when they got out of line, but after being in this hellhole, those days were surely over. I would put a nigga down in an instant, just like I did when I was on the street. The only difference was, I would be using my shank instead of my gun.

"Alright, cuz, call my jack if you need anything." He gave me a hug and headed toward the exit.

This jail shit had turned me into a cold-hearted individual from all the fucked-up stories I heard, all the bullshit I had to endure, and the new life I struggled to survive. Everything was as good as it could get behind bars, and then it happened.

Chapter Five

————————

Dynesha lay in bed butt naked, staring at the ceiling, while the young hustler knelt between her legs, sucking on her clit. His head game was trash, and she couldn't wait for it to be over. This was the second time they linked up this week, and she only let him eat the pussy. Sex was not an option, even if he offered her a million dollars. She only did it because he paid like he weighed, and the nigga was fat as fuck. Nothing about him turned her on.

"Oh shit, daddy, your tongue is the shit," she lied, pinching her nipples.

He stood up and pulled down his sweat-pants, revealing his penis. Dynesha almost laughed in his face when she saw the size of it. It had to be the littlest thing she had ever seen.

"Whoa, we can't do that. I told you nothing can go in me until after my gynecologist appoint-ment. Trust me, daddy, it will be worth the wait," she said, stroking all five inches of his manhood.

"How about you get on your knees and suck my dick," he said, sitting at the edge of the bed.

When she didn't move quick enough, the fat fuck smacked her off the bed. Dynesha hit the floor hard, blood leaking from the side of her mouth.

"What you think, you just gonna keep taking my money and not give me any pussy? You have two choices, spread those legs and take some of this good dick, or get down here and let me see what your head game is like."

Dynesha was so in shock from the sudden change, that she didn't realize her twin sister had entered the room. They would watch each other's back just in case something like this happened. Rynesha had her .25 aimed at the young boy's face.

"You like putting your fat, dick-beating hands on my sister?" she asked, ready to pop off if he made any sudden moves. He looked over at the nightstand where his gun was, but didn't try to reach for it. Rynesha also looked. "I dare you, dumb ass, do it."

He could tell that she meant business, and didn't move. Rynesha came closer to her sister, who was now standing, putting her clothes back on. The hustler stared at both women, wondering what they were about to do. Were they trying to rob him? That would be a mistake on their end, because he would kill both of them and wouldn't lose a night's sleep over it.

"So what you little bitches gonna do, huh? Rob me? Here, take the dough, but you better watch your back," he stated, pulling a knot of money from his pocket and tossing it on the bed.

"Tie his ass up, Dy," Rynesha told her sister.

She tied the hustler's arms and legs to the frame of the bed, using the sheets. After making sure he couldn't move, Dynesha picked the money up and tucked it away.

"You got what your whore ass wanted, now run."

"Nigga, it ain't that simple," Dynesha replied, digging in her purse and removing a hunting knife. "You put your hands on me. Don't no nigga put their hands on me or my sister."

The sight of the blade had him bitching up. All that tough shit he was spitting earlier, now turned into him pleading not to get cut. Dynesha stood over the man, holding the knife in one hand and gripping his penis with the other. The more he tried squirming out of her grasp, the tighter her grip got. Rynesha watched on in total horror, knowing what her sister was about to do.

She always said she wanted to Angela Bobbitt somebody.

"Get the fuck off of me, bitch," he yelled.

In one swift motion, Dynesha sliced, severing his dick from his body. The pain was so excruciating, that he went in to shock and passed out. Rynesha aimed her weapon at his head and fired two rounds at point-blank range. The bullets left brain matter all over the remaining bedsheets. Gathering any and every thing that may incriminate them, they left the hotel room, jumped in their vehicle, and fled the scene.

"Bitch, you are really fucking crazy," Rynesha said, sparking up the dutch.

"Bitch, I know." She smiled, holding up the hustler's severed penis in her gloved hand.

A couple of blocks away from the hotel, Dynesha tossed the piece of meat out the window along with the bloody gloves. Out of the three sisters, she was the most dangerous. One of the many men she dealt with had taught her all about the game and all of the many obstacles she would face. He practically raised her by way of the streets and taught her how to defend herself. Murder became second nature to

Dynesha. Everything she learned, she taught her twin sister, so they would always have each other's back. She tried including Karma, but she had a different agenda. She wanted to be the educated one of the three.

She ended up going to college and getting her degree in law. She was now working in a small criminal law firm in Carbondale, as an interim. They specialized in certain cases that needed special attention. Although she was still considered a newbie, she played a very valuable role on their six-man team. Karma hoped that one day she would become a partner.

When the twins got home, Karma was sitting at the kitchen table watching some breaking news on the TV while finishing her brief that was due in court tomorrow. One look at them, and she knew that they had gotten into something bad.

"What have you bitches been up to?"

"Nothing!" Rynesha was the first to speak.

"That don't look like nothing," Karma said, pointing at the TV screen. She knew her sisters all too well, and it only took a second to know they were behind the murder.

"The nigga got out of line, so he had to be dealt with," Dynesha chimed in, knowing that their baby sister wasn't stupid.

"What happened? I want to know every-thing."

"No, sis! The less you know, the better," Rynesha said, grabbing the pitcher of juice out of the refrigerator. "All we need you to do is keep working at that law firm just in case we need you to get us out of this mess."

"Don't worry about that. I got you, but I still need to know just in case I need to do my research. With all the new technology, it's really hard to get away with shit. So start talking," Karma said, giving her sisters her undivided attention.

~ ~ ~

The next morning, Karma sat in the conference room with her bosses, going over case after case trying to find loopholes in the prosecutions witness. This case was extra sensitive to Karma because it was someone she had grown an interest in over the last few years. Although she wasn't going to be second chair, she would make sure she was right there to see it through. There were a couple of discrepancies which ended up causing the judge to order an immediate hearing.

Karma sat in the back of the courtroom so she couldn't be seen, listening to the judge as he made his final decision on the case. Her heart felt like it was pounding through her chest.

"Even though without a shadow of doubt, there was substantially a crime committed, the officers in this case did some things that I find disturbing," the judge began. "However, as a sworn officer of the court, I still have an obligation to review all the facts. This is a hard decision but I'm going to deny the defendant's appeal."

Karma's mouth dropped open when she heard the judge's decision. The whole court-room suddenly went into an uproar. The judge banged his gavel trying to restore order. Karma stood up with a disappointed look on her face and headed for the door. She was just about to walk out when the judge started talking again.

"As I was saying before the interruption," he said, staring at the defendant, "I'm denying your appeal, but I'm going to show you some compassion in the matter. With that said, it is in the best interest of this court and the legal system to suspend the remainder of your sentence with the exception of the probation."

The courtroom erupted again, but this time with cheers. There were only about fifteen people in the room, but you would have thought it was full to capacity. Karma stopped, turned around, and watched the reaction of the rest of her team. Even they were surprised by what they heard.

"When you are released, make sure you report straight to your probation officer to go over what you're allowed and not allowed to do," the judge finished. "I don't ever want to see you in my courtroom again, or it won't be a pleasant reunion."

The defendant nodded and smiled before being escorted back to the holding cell. Karma and the rest of the legal team left the Lackawanna County Courthouse with a wonderful victory that morning. A celebration was definitely in the making. She called her sisters as she headed back to the office.

"What, bitch?" Dynesha answered on the third ring.

"Whatever, let's go to Levels tonight. We won a case that had a lot to do with my research.

That might get me in the courtroom as second chair next. Maybe even first soon," Karma said excitedly.

"Congratulations, lil sis. I'll let Rynesha know when she get out the shower."

"Okay, see you when I get home."

Karma ended the call and pumped her fist in the air. To her, this was a big-time win. If she would have realized the storm that was brewing, she would have packed an umbrella.

Chapter Six

───────

It might sound crazy, but after being in a state prison for fifty-one months, five days, eleven hours, thirty-six minutes, and however many seconds, my whole perception of the world had changed. The streets didn't look or feel the same. The shit felt harsh, making me feel like an outsider. I felt like a stray dog with no place to call home. One thing that I wasn't going to do was go home and be treated like a baby, begging for some bitch to take me back. Since being in prison, Abby had cut me off just like everyone else. I hadn't even heard from her in the last two years. It turned me into a cold individual.

During the first couple of days, I almost fucked around and went back to prison. I went to see my parole agent, and he tried to flex on me from the rip. He said I was lying about what took me so long to get to his office, and that the address I gave him was a vacant home that the police had just removed trespassers from earlier that day.

"There has to be some mistake. This was the address I was at before going to prison."

"Just get me an address before the end of the week," he snapped.

He went over the rest of my release conditions, then said the first time I fucked up, he would be right there to slap the cuffs on my wrist.

"I don't plan on ever seeing another prison cell again," I told him, walking out of his office.

"We'll see about that," he yelled out, typing something on his computer.

After leaving my PO's office, I went past my block to see what had happened to my old apartment. When I got to the corner of Webster Street, the apartment building I use to stay in was abandoned and boarded up. It looked like it had been that way for a while now. Old beer bottles covered the driveway, and there was trash from a turned-over trashcan all over the yard. I wondered what happened to all my stuff that was in there.

"Hey, I remember you," someone said, causing me to turn around. It was my old neighbor from down the street. "I told my wife that was you."

"How are you, Mr. Jamison?" I shook his hand.

"Jordan, it's nice to see they let you out. I hope it was an eye-opener and you leave that mess alone, son. God has a mysterious way of showing his love for you. Don't take it for granted this time."

Mr. Jamison was a very religious man. Him and his family stayed in church every Sunday. He had two daughters and a son. The oldest one had gone off to college while I was incarcerated. She was one of those stuck-up kids that never got into trouble. Her dad made sure she stayed away from all the neighborhood boys that constantly tried to get with her. She was daddy's girl. Now he was here preaching to me about walking a straight path. The crazy part about it was, I was listening.

I haven't seen any of my friends since hitting the streets, but I heard they were out here getting plenty of money. I only had $230 left that I came home with. My PO only gave me a couple of days to give him an address or who knows what he would try to do. I couldn't use the $40 a night hotel I was staying at because it was only temporary. As long as I was on probation, I was going to try to do the right thing.

"Mr. Jamison I will talk to you later. I have to go fill out some papers to get my medical card."

"I'm heading that way, I'll drop you off," he said, hitting the alarm on his Chevy Tahoe.

"Thank you, I'll give you gas money," I offered.

"I don't need any gas money," he replied, flagging off my offer.

I hopped out of the car at the welfare office and thanked Mr. Jamison for the ride. He shook my hand tightly and slid me $300 from the palm of his hand.

"This should hold you over until you get on your feet. Come over Sunday; one of my nieces is coming over to cook dinner for us."

I thanked him for the money and the invite, then headed inside the welfare office. It only took about thirty minutes to fill out the paperwork and make an appointment to get my medical and access card. I walked down to the Steamtown Mall to find something to wear. I needed to get out of the clothes I'd been wearing for the last couple of days. As I was walking in the door, some fat white boy was trying to force his way out past me like I wasn't there. We bumped into each other hard.

"Watch where the fuck you going, nigga," he said, sizing me up.

"Who you talking to?" I shot back, knowing he was talking to me.

He swelled up like he was ready to pop off. He must have not known that I was all about that violent shit. I didn't want to draw too much attention because I would surely end up right back in prison if I came into any contact with the police. I told him to meet me in the mall parking lot. I was walking behind him, but noticed he was heading toward his car. This dumb-ass white boy must have been stupid if he thought I was going to allow him make it to his car to get a weapon.

I snuck up on him from behind and cracked him so hard that he hit the ground. I cocked my fist back and stood over him. He tried to kick me, but I side stepped it and kicked him in the face. For the next two minutes, I worked his fat ass out like I was his personal trainer. By the time I was done, I had left him leaking facedown on the ground next to his wheel.

~ ~ ~

Sunday came fast, and I decided to take Mr.

Jamison's offer on dinner. After eating McDonald's and other takeout, a home-cooked meal was just what I needed. When I stepped into his crib, it took me by surprise how well decorated and furnished it was. I always thought of Mr. Jamison as the cheap type, but not anymore.

"Have a seat, son. My niece and wife are setting the table for us now," Mr. Jamison told me.

"Thank you again for everything," I said, sitting on the couch.

We talked for a few more minutes before Mrs. Jamison came in and told us dinner was ready. I followed them into the dining room and took a seat across from them. Sitting to my left was probably the most beautiful female I had ever seen. She looked so familiar to me, I just couldn't pinpoint it right off hand. She looked like a thick slice of heaven on earth. She had this warmth about her, with a light skin tone to match. She wasn't naked; her complexion was visible only because her face and hands were exposed. From the neck down, she was fully dressed. She wore a cocaine-white fitted shirt with khaki-colored slacks. Her hourglass shape seeped through her clothes, giving her a sexy professional look. Besides all that, something about her was screaming *hood*.

That might be the reason she was wearing nonprescription glasses, to hide her true side. The more I tried to figure out where I knew her from, the more I strained my brain. Her eyes were round and slanted toward the ends like commas. For a second, I got lost in their glow. Her come-kiss-me lips and her visible dimples made my dick jump.

It wasn't the animal reaction that surprised me, it was the feeling she made me feel in my heart that did. I don't know why, but the sight of her made me want to love every part of her, inside and out. She was the type that made a nigga want to go out and hustle hard, just to spoil her.

"Hello, Jordan," she said while staring into my eyes. "I'm glad you finally made it home."

Not only did she know my name, but she also knew that I was locked up. Who is she? As we ate, I kept glancing over at her, admiring her beautiful smile. The longer I stared at her, the more I wanted to wrap her long ponytail around my hand and pull on it until it made her head tilt back so I could place soft kisses up and down her smooth neck, which I bet was perfumed.

"Do I know you? You look so familiar."

"Sure you know me. We met at the club years ago before you went inside," she finally stated. "You were with your boo."

I thought back to that day, hoping I could put her face with a name. Then it hit me. I knew this wasn't the shorty me and my boys bought drinks for. What was her name?

"Karma?"

She gave me the most seductive smile I had ever seen, confirming her identity. I damn near fell out of my chair at the sight of this fine specimen.

"You look even better than you did back then."

"That's because I grew up, have a job, and am taking care of myself."

"You two know each other?" Mrs. Jamison asked.

"We met briefly, Auntie," Karma replied. She playfully elbowed me in my side.

Her touch was so gentle and soft that it left me wanting to feel it again. I wanted to find out just how much of her body was as soft as her touch. I almost didn't eat my food from watching her move her fork in and out of her mouth. The shit was erotic as fuck. If it wasn't for my pants, I think my dick would've broken through the table. I turned to my plate, and immediately the food blocked out my thoughts of Karma.

We all laughed and joked over our meal, and it made me miss being back in Philly with my family and friends. Karma was the life of the party. She made sure silence never found a seat at the table. She told me about her two sisters and how crazy they were, but never told me they were twins. I would find that out later. The atmosphere made me feel like I was part of their family and not some dude that just came home from prison that they felt sorry for.

Once we finished eating, we went back into the living room and watched the season premiere of *Claws*. I wanted to know more about Karma, and I could tell she wanted the same. We talked and enjoyed each other's company until Mr. and Mrs. Jamison got tired.

"Karma, can you give Jordan a ride back to the hotel on your way home?" Mr. Jamison asked.

"Sure!"

~ ~ ~

She hit the alarm to her white Mercedes Benz and sat in the driver's seat. It fucked me up to see her driving something like that, but it also turned me on. I opened up the passenger door and hopped in. The first thing I noticed when I looked in her direction was her pussy print poking out from the khakis. That made my dick try to break out of captivity. I wanted to have some of that. Thinking we shared the same mutual interest, I leaned over and tried to kiss her. That instantly flipped the switch on her.

"Whoa, it ain't that kind of party."

"Come on, beautiful, I know you want this too," I said, leaning in again trying to get a kiss. She pushed me back hard this time.

"Look, Jordan, you can save all that 'beautiful' shit for some other bitch. I have a man. Furthermore, I don't need you to compliment me on my looks or my intelligence, because I already know my worth." She took her hair out of the ponytail holder and shook it until her hair relaxed on her shoulders before continuing. "My uncle asked me to help you get an apartment because my man has plenty. We could never hook up now. You blew that chance when you failed to say you had a girl. I would have surely gave you some pussy back then, but that shit is over now."

I was lost for words. I wanted to say something that would cut her like her words had cut me, but I didn't know what the fuck to say. Her whole demeanor had changed since we got in her car. Was it just a front for her peoples? Damn, was she that mad about me having a girl and not coming at her? Where was all this anger coming from? What did she mean by her uncle asked her to help me get a roof over my head? I didn't need her or her man. I decided to give her a piece of what she had dished out, because I could tell she wasn't used to getting any of it back.

"Calm down before you let your mouth kill your looks, sweetheart! I didn't know you felt like that or that I was invited over here tonight so you could help me."

"Don't talk to me like—"

I cut her off and continued, "If I knew that's what this was, I would've made sure I didn't show up tonight. I'm not looking for charity. I lost everything when I went to prison, but I'd sleep in the streets before I'd make kissing your snobby ass a priority. I told you that you were beautiful back then because you were. I said it a few minutes ago before you opened up that nasty-ass mouth you got, and at the time you were to me. But I take it back now!"

"What, you mad cause I'm not going to fuck you?" she snapped back. I ignored her and finished what I had to say.

"And about you having intelligence, I don't recall ever saying that, because you showing me right now you dumb as fuck if you thought that's all I wanted from you." I opened the car door and stepped out. I bent down to speak again. "Thanks but no thanks for the ride; I'll walk back to the hotel. By the way, sweetheart, you ain't as perfect as you think you are. You have greens stuck in your off-white-ass teeth!"

I slammed her door shut and left her sitting there, silent. As bad as she was, I couldn't just let her say what she wanted to me and get away with it. She didn't know nothing about me, and with how funky her attitude was, she wouldn't ever get to.

Chapter Seven

City Girls' "That's My Type" played in the background as Rynesha and Dynesha took turns deep throating the young hustler's medium-size dick. They had traveled all the way out to Delaware to trick some hustler they had been messaging on Instagram. He shot Rynesha a message in her DM, and she immediately responded telling him that she would visit that weekend. He didn't know that he was getting a package deal with her sister tagging along. It was his fantasy to fuck twins, and now he was living out that fantasy in the flesh.

They both wore cheerleader outfits without any panties. The tops of the outfits were tight and thin, clinging to their erect nipples that poked through the fabric. The skirts were so short that even if they could cross their legs, you could still see their clean-shaven pussies, leaving nothing to the imagination. They continued giving him the best head he ever had.

Sluuurrrp! Sluuurrrp! Sluuurrrp! Damn, papi,

you have a big dick," Dynesha lied.

"So you like this dick, huh?" he said with confidence. "Wait until I plug up that little pussy of yours."

"You sure you can handle all this good good?" Rynesha asked, spreading her legs, giving him a view of her clit that poked out from her pussy lips.

"Strip," he said.

He watched them undress each other, with shy glances and coquettish looks at him, peeling off each other's tops and shimmying out of their skirts. Their bodies were identical, from their fine tits and taut bellies, to their nice firm asses. He felt like he would cum just from watching them.

"I want to watch y'all perform."

Rynesha and her twin sister put one hand on each other's hip, slipping the other hand into the other's wet cunt, fingering each other. They tilted their faces together, eyes closed, and kissed, lips parted, their tongues moving gently in sync as he watched stroking himself.

He slipped off his pants and boxers and sat back down, continuing to stroke himself while they made out. It was the best performance he had ever seen.

"Pinch her nipples," he said, and Dynesha reached out and tweaked, making a moan escape from Rynesha's throat. "Harder!"

Dynesha twisted, but her sister didn't make any sounds of pain, just sounds of enjoyment. It only excited the hustler even more. He couldn't wait to sink his erection into both of them. The two women got on all fours, lowering their heads to the carpet, leaving their asses in the air. He started squeezing their asses, occasionally rubbing their assholes with his fingers. They moaned and moved against his touch as he slipped a finger inside. Dynesha came seconds later, causing her body to convulse and fall to the floor.

He got behind Rynesha and slipped his dick into her, making her body tense just a bit while continuing to finger Dynesha. She quickly adjusted and accepted his girth without making a sound. When he was close to an orgasm, he pulled out. Both women turned around and looked at him worshipfully, licking their lips, as he tugged at his dick until he shot cum onto their smiling faces.

Once spent, he sat back on the lounge chair, feeling empty. Dynesha was in a rush to get hers, so she crawled over between his legs, grabbed his limp dick, and began sucking slowly, almost meditatively, on the head until he was hard again. He pushed her back onto the floor and placed his head between her legs.

While tonguing her clit, he stuck a finger inside her causing her to let out a loud gasp. His tongue was working magic on her, but she was ready to get fucked.

"Let me see what you working with," she moaned, pushing him over and then swinging one leg over to straddle him, and eased herself down, guiding his dick into her hole.

She rocked on top of him, reaching down to steady her pace by holding on to his chest. She slipped one of her fingers into his mouth.

"Damn, y'all some freaks," he managed to get out his mouth before Rynesha sat on his face.

A euphoria grew inside him, spread through his body, suffusing his limbs with outrushing lightness. He had never felt this good before. While Rynesha rode his face, Dynesha rode his dick. The two gave each other a smile as if they knew what each other was thinking. Rynesha came for the second time in his mouth, then got off of him. She headed in the bathroom to wash up.

Dynesha lowered herself, breasts against his chest, cheek against his cheek, her breath in his ear, and he reached down to take hold of her ass with both hands. He thrust his hips against her, and her breath quickened as she thrust back, and soon they were rocking together until he felt himself about to cum. He squeezed her ass harder and shot his load inside her. She gasped in his ear and shuddered, trembling to her own orgasm. It shot out of her and onto his pelvic area. It was a mixture of both semens, dripping all over him as she went to stand up.

"I need a shower," Dynesha said, heading toward the bathroom.

"Wait for me," the hustler replied, getting off the floor. "I'm going to join you."

"No, you stay here. We have something else special for you."

Getting excited again the hustler lay down on the bed and waited for the two sisters to finish what they were doing. He sparked up a dutch and took a couple of pulls, then closed his eyes, letting out the smoke. As he went to take another pull, he felt something cold touching his balls. When he opened his eyes, the dutch fell out of his mouth and onto the floor.

"What the fuck is you doing with that?" he asked, confused.

Rynesha was standing there with her gun aimed at his genitals. Dynesha was already making her way across the room for the safe that they knew was in the closet. They had watched him grab money out of it earlier when he was trying to impress them, thinking that they were some average tricks.

"You know what it is. What's the comb-ination?" Rynesha asked. When he didn't answer fast enough, she took the butt of the gun and whacked him in his balls. The pain was excruciating. "What's the number, nigga?"

"You a crumb-ass bitch," he moaned, holding his nut sack. Rynesha raised her hand to swing again, but he copped out. "Wait, wait! It's 21-16-34."

Dynesha typed the numbers into the keypad, and the safe popped open. There were stacks of money lined up in the front. She quickly grabbed a pillowcase and started loading the money up. When she reach in the back of the safe, she came across about ten packages wrapped in brown paper bags. A smile came over her face, knowing what was wrapped inside.

"We hit the jackpot, Sis," she yelled, placing the packages inside the pillowcase.

"Now that wasn't so hard, was it?" Rynesha said, grinning at the hustler. "Next time, don't bring some bitches you don't know to your crib, especially when you're carrying that much shit."

"Let's roll, Ry."

They tied the hustler's hands together, grabbed the rest of their shit, and headed for the door. Dynesha hit the alarm on her SUV and hopped in the driver seat. After placing the pillowcases in the backseat, Rynesha went to reach for the passenger-side door, when gun shots erupted. She ducked down trying to dodge the bullets. Dynesha scanned the parking lot and noticed the hustler running down the steps firing wildly in their direction. She grabbed her weapon, firing back at him, to give her sister time to get in the vehicle.

"Hurry up and get us out of here," Rynesha yelled, closing the door and ducking down.

"I'm trying," Dynesha snapped back. She put the SUV in drive and hit the gas, speeding out of the parking complex as bullets continued flying, shattering their back window.

~ ~ ~

"Can I get a chicken wing platter, with fried rice?"

"Anything else?" the Chinese lady asked, writing down my order.

"No, that will be all."

It had been three weeks since the altercation with Karma had taken place. I hadn't heard from or seen her or her uncle since then. I grabbed my food and went back to my hotel room to relax. There was trash everywhere that I had left over the last couple of days because I was running the streets. I wondered why housekeeping didn't come clean up yet. I hated being in this hellhole, but I had no place to go yet. I still hadn't talked to anyone yet.

As I was listening to music and working out, I thought I heard a knock on the door to my room. The knocks got harder. I walked over and opened the door. Standing there, looking plain as hell in some black sweatpants and as extra tight white T-shirt and scuffed-up black running shoes, and with no glasses on, was Karma, with bags in both hands.

"What's up?" I asked as drily as fuck, blocking her entrance into my room. If she wanted a do-over, she was going to have to humble herself and beg for one.

"I had stopped by to check on my aunt, and my uncle asked if I could drop these clothes off to you."

"Thanks!" I said, snatching the bags out of her hands and then forcefully closing the door in her face.

I hit fifty more push-ups to give her time to leave, then peeped through the window to make sure she was gone, but she wasn't. She was standing by her car, pulling her hair up in a ponytail. I thought she wanted to fight or something. I laughed at the thought of her coming back up here and swinging on me. She grabbed a large folder from the backseat and headed back toward my door. I ran to the bathroom so she wouldn't know I was standing by the window watching her. Hopefully she didn't see the curtain shaking. I made her knock three times before I snatched the door open like I was irritated.

"What now, Karma?"

"Damn, you don't have to say it like that. I have to show you something."

"I'm busy."

"Busy doing what in this dirty-ass room?" she snapped. "All I need is like ten minutes of your time."

"Just doing me, shorty. I have roaches and rats up in here. I don't want your prissy ass to be all scared and shit. You know how beneath you I am." I chuckled, trying to sound as corny as I possibly could.

"That's why I pulled my hair up and wore these clothes," she countered, rolling her eyes at me. "I don't care about this stuff. I'm going to burn them and take a flea bath when I leave here, so move out of my way."

She pushed me out of the way like she was running shit. I was kind of turned on by her aggressiveness, but I would never let her know it. She was disgusted by the way my room looked, and it was all over her face. I was surprised when she grabbed a trash bag and started picking up the garbage off the floor. After filling up the trash bag, she sealed it and headed out the door.

Karma came back a few minutes later with

an armful of clean bedding and cleaning supplies, which I could tell belonged to the hotel. She put on some plastic gloves and went to work. She didn't ask what was trash or what I wanted to keep. She just took it upon herself to throw shit away. Karma didn't say a word after she started cleaning, and feeling like I wasn't helping, I joined in. When the room was spotless, she finally spoke.

"Are you ready to take a look at some stuff? I'm sorry, but my mind doesn't function well around filth."

Karma didn't know it, but she had just reeled me in, and I was going to make her bougie ass fall in love with me one way or the other.

Chapter Eight

———

"How the fuck you let yourself get caught
up? Then you don't contact me for damn near a
month, like you were hiding or something."

"Man, I didn't see that shit coming. I think
they put something in my drink, and I wasn't
ducking you," Jake lied, not trying to let him
know that he had blatantly fucked up. "And I
didn't say anything because just needed some
time to try and find them."

"Did you find them yet?"

"No, but I'm going to."

"You better find these bitches and get my
shit back, or someone will be paying you a visit.
You have two weeks to do so."

"I'm trying to but—"

The line went dead, leaving Jake with a
puzzled look on his face. One thing for certain,
he would not be taking that threat for granted.
He knew all too well how deadly muthafuckas
got over their bread. He downed a couple of
niggas himself for coming up short. Jake took a
quick shower, then changed into a pair of black

True Religion jeans and a pair of all-black Timbs. He needed to find out where those bitches were resting and put a bullet in both of their heads. He periodically kept going back to the club in Wilmington where he first met them, but they weren't there or were just in hiding. He called his man to see what he was doing.

"Yo, bull!" Hot Dog said, answering on the forth ring. "I heard what happened to you. Why are you just now hitting me up? That was the first thing I heard when I came home. Nobody didn't say shit when I called. How you let them bitches get the drop on you like that?"

"Well for one, you were doing your bid, so you couldn't do shit for me in there. And I think they slipped me something that knocked me the fuck out," he lied again. "You know they wouldn't have done shit to me if I wasn't in a comatose state of mind."

"So how do you want to handle this?"

"I got a call a few minutes ago from my supplier."

"And?"

"What you think, nigga? He gave me two weeks to get his shit back or come up with his money, or he's sending them boys after me,"

Jake replied nervously.

"Damn," Hot Dog said. "Well you know I'm rocking with you no matter what. I have to turn myself back in next month, but fuck them. Catch me if they can. Let's find these bitches and get your shit back. Where do we start?"

~ ~ ~

Karma had left me a stack of information on places where I could go to help me with housing, and help-wanted ads. She was an advocate for the homeless people whenever she wasn't saving innocent people that were falsely accused of criminal behavior. She really knew what she was talking about, too, when it came to getting people off the street. As I read through the folder she left me, I realized there was no way I would be caught staying at some of those places. It made me want to hustle harder to ensure that I wouldn't end up in one. Luckily for me, I found a job at Teaser's Nightclub, making thirteen dollars an hour.

The Jamisons had become like family to me, and once I figured out how to make their niece fall in love with me, we'd hopefully be related by marriage. I was learning Karma, and one of the lessons she had unknowingly taught me was that she didn't respect niceness. She would walk right over it and leave you lying there feeling vulnerable. I had learned that much about her in the little time we were around each other, and I'd be damned if I made that mistake twice.

A couple of days before, I had mentioned to Mr. Jamison that my birthday was coming up this week. Karma overheard me and asked what I was doing. I changed the subject, and she didn't like it.

"Why are you trying to be so secretive about your birthday? You must be about to get into something you have no business doing."

"Naw. I'll just be chilling," I replied.

"Chilling how, Jordan?" I shrugged my shoulders. "I'm asking because if you don't have any major plans, I'd like to take you to get something to eat or something."

"I'll let you know what's up."

I waited until the day before my birthday to call her and tell her that we could go out. A part of me didn't want to go because I didn't have money like that to be paying for anyone but myself. Plus, I didn't like women paying for meals when we went out. After going back and forth with her about my finances and what a man was supposed to do, we agreed on her cooking for me at her place.

Karma picked me up around six o'clock because I told her I had to go see my PO early in the morning. She was looking amazing. She had on a tight, all-black, ankle-length strapless dress and some red-and-black heels, with a red purse to match. Her hair was flowing straight down her back, and she smelled like she had on some expensive perfume. She was too dressed up to just be cooking at the house.

I wasn't looking too bad myself in an all-black button-down with black slacks and butter Timberland boots, compliments of Mr. Jamison. The clothes he had bought me were very nice. He had good taste for an old man.

"Where are we going?"

"You'll see." She laughed.

We jumped on 81 heading south and ended up in Wilkes-Barre, in Bear Creek, at the casino. I didn't have to say anything because my facial expression said it all.

"Wait. Before we go in, I got you something."

She went to her trunk and took out an

envelope and a huge bag full of stuff.

"What is that?"

"It's for your birthday," she said, handing me the card. "And this is for your new job."

I opened up the card, and there were five crisp hundred-dollar bills in it. Before I could protest, she covered her ears and closed her eyes, smiling.

"You gotta have money to gamble with and take me out to eat afterward."

"You're a fucking nut, girl. What's in this bag?"

When I opened the bag up, there were two brand-new white dress shirts, two black vests, two pairs of black dress pants, dress socks, and a pair of dress shoes.

"I thought you'd need them, working in a strip club and all."

I leaned down and kissed her on the cheek, then grabbed her by the hand and led her through the casino doors.

"Come on, we got money to win."

The casino wasn't ready for a nigga like me, or a beautiful lady like Karma. In my first fifteen minutes, I hit for $1,800 on the slot machines and was ready to get up out of there. I handed

Karma eight hundred, and she refused to accept it.

"No, that's your birthday gift! I don't want it back."

"You gave me five. I'm giving you eight. All I'm doing is splitting my winnings with you."

"I don't want any of the money you won. In your situation, you need the money way more than I do."

"I was wondering when you were going to show your true colors. In my situation, huh? You mean me being broke and homeless, living in a fucking hotel room? I've been looking at you as a friend, but now I know what it is. I'm another homeless-ass nigga on your caseload."

"I didn't mean it like that, Jordan," she snapped back, giving me a look that if they could kill, I would be dead.

"So how did you mean it then, Queen Karma, Goddess of Scranton?" She didn't answer my question because she couldn't. Her silence let me know that this was just her doing her advocacy work. I dropped the money on her lap. "Here! That's for the uniforms you got me and the five you gave. Keep the change, so you can buy yourself something to eat. This ain't a date.

I'm not paying for your shit. Remember, I'm a broke-ass nigga that came home from prison with nothing."

The hurt she wore looked good on her face. I walked away from the slots and left her sitting there to think about what she had done. She found me a few minutes later, feeding my face at the casino's buffet.

"I'm sorry, Jordan. I swear I didn't mean it that way. Yes, you're in a messed-up situation with everyone taking all your money and leaving you with nothing, but I'm not your advocate, nor am I your caseworker. I'm here with you, celebrating your birthday as your friend."

"I bet."

"I am! How can I look down on you when I once was in your shoes?"

"I doubt you were ever in my shoes, not the way you act."

"How do I act?"

"Like an uppity-ass, spoiled bitch that ain't been through any real shit to humble your ass."

Karma sat in the seat next to mine and moved in so close to me that our legs touched.

"You need to watch that 'bitch' word. You damn right, I'm spoiled by me! What you don't know is that I've earned the right to act like this. Me and my sisters crawled before we walked. They may have not chosen the path that I did, but we did what we had to do to survive. While they ran the streets having fun, my mother kept me in the house studying to be what I am today. My mother busted her ass to provide for us, and my sisters returned the favor in their own way. As for me, now I'm sprinting, and soon you'll be doing the same. I became a paralegal, and I worked in this field as a constant reminder of where I've been and how, if I fall off and stop doing what's right, I could be right back there. Everything I've seen in the past and present has humbled me, but I'm not going to walk around here like I'm weak."

I could tell from the first time I met her that her eyes held a story that she needed to get out, but here wasn't the place. Before she spilled her guts in the overcrowded buffet, I placed my index finger over her mouth.

"Let's go somewhere else and talk."

We rode back to my room, listening to the sounds of Jeremiah's "Love Don't Change." Not a word was spoken the whole way. Everything about Karma was unpredictable except her attitude. She walked in my room and kicked off her heels, then sat on my bed.

"Hand me those pizza delivery papers off the table. Everybody didn't get to eat at the buffet like you," she said, sitting cross-legged, with a pillow propped behind her back and another on her lap.

I handed them to her and asked her to order a stromboli for me as well, along with some cheese fries with extra cheese.

"Sure! What kind do you want? I'm going to get a pizza for myself. I hope you know you're paying for it, friend. This ain't no date!"

She smiled at me with her last words, and I felt myself melting away. The sadness had left from her face, and I was happy to see it gone.

"You need to fix your mouth, baby girl. As a matter of fact, come here so I can fix it for you!" Karma didn't move. "Come here."

"If you want to fix my mouth, you'll need to come to me."

"Is that right, smart ass? Then I guess it will just have to stay funky, but you know what that means, don't you?"

"What does it mean?" She had a flirtatious smile on her face.

"We can't be friends no more. I don't have friendships with people that have funky mouths." I folded my arms and turned my back to her, like a small child ending a friendship.

Karma started laughing, but her laugh was getting closer to me, until it tickled the hairs on the back of my neck. She turned me around, unfolded my arms, and softly kissed me on the lips.

"Then I guess we can't be friends, and since we ain't dating, like you've announced all night, I guess you'll just have to settle for being my man."

We kissed and grabbed, letting our hands roam all over each other's bodies. She tried to snatch my shirt open like some shit seen in a movie, but only one button broke. We both fell out laughing, instantly killing the mood. I lifted my shirt over my head but left my muscle shirt on, and then I took her hand in mine. I led her to the wooden chair at the table and sat in it. I lifted her dress up, revealing a black thong, and made her straddle my lap.

Common sense seemed to kick in for the first time, and before we could go any further with what we were about to do, we needed to talk.

"Look at me, beautiful." I cupped her chin in my hand gently turning her face until we were eye to eye. "Do you know what you're saying and who you're saying it to? Look around you. This is all a nigga got."

"I know what you got. You got everything in this room."

Karma reached in with her lips to kiss me, but I turned my head, so her kiss landed on my cheek. She was talking with her pussy. I could feel the heat and dampness through my slacks. I needed to talk to her heart and mind. If what she was saying to me was real, I'd have time to talk to her second set of lips later.

"I'm serious, Karma. I don't have a car to come see you in, or a cellphone to call you on. I don't have anything I need to keep a relationship afloat, but if you believe in me like the shit you said about me crawling and sprinting, and are willing to give me time, I'll have all that. In time, I'll be able to give you everything you need and then some, but you can't break bad on me during the struggle."

"Jordan, you're talking too serious for me," she said, getting off my lap. "I know what you're saying, but it sounds like moving in together, marriage, and kids to me. I'm not ready for none of that right now. I just want to take things slow and get to know each other better."

"I hear what you're saying, but to me, it sounds like you saying you can't be faithful." I joined her in standing up. As she looked up into my eyes, I looked down into hers.

"I can be faithful, but I've been hurt before, badly. My sisters told me never to let a nigga hurt me again. I can't be as cold-hearted as they are though. I'm feeling you, everything about you. I'm feeling your brown eyes, your toned body, and those firm-ass lips."

Everything she said was physical. Where was all the other shit, like me being smart, funny, or fucking caring?

"If all I wanted was a nut, Karma, there's this little thick-ass bitch next door selling pussy. She already said she'd give me a discount for being her neighbor."

"Stop playing with me, Jordan," she replied, thumping me in my mouth. "If all I wanted to do was get fucked, I'd find me a nigga with money to pay for my services. A wet pussy and a dry purse don't match, feel me? You better not laugh at what I'm about to say to you, and don't judge me. I wanted you ever since we met at that club. When I found out that you went to prison, I used to have wet dreams about you. When we met again at my aunt's house and you said all that disrespectful shit to me in the car, I knew I had to have you. I've never had a man keep it that real with me, and that's exactly what I've been looking for."

She laughed and grabbed both of my hands and then stood on her tippy toes until her lips were so close to my ear, I could feel her breathing.

"I knew you were the one man that would be able to tame me and teach me how to trust again. All I ask of you is not to break my heart."

I took her dress off and scooped her up from the floor. I cut my mind off and let my soul control my movements. I kissed every dry spot on her body and tongue-kissed every place that contained moisture. After twenty minutes or so of listening to her beg through moans, I gave her what she'd been asking for. I dipped in and pulled right back out to release. I wasn't prepared for what she had to offer, and it was my first nut as a free man, but I didn't need a pill this time to get back up. As fast as my release came, I was ready for my second trip to uncharted waters.

Her grip, combined with the warm wetness, sent chills up my spine with each stroke. I shook with every thrust as if I was locked in a freezer, but she was on fire. Karma moved her body like a gymnast, as evidenced by the way she rested her knees on her shoulders to welcome all of my dick inside her wet pussy.

I accepted the welcome and slid in until her body made me stop and my balls prevented me from diving deeper. When I freed her breasts from her bra to pacify my mouth, a condom fell onto the bed. I grabbed it and showed it to her.

"Wishful thinking?" she said, shrugging her shoulders.

I applied the rubber, which I should have done from the start, then slid back in. The sensation to bust had calmed down, and it was on. With a mouthful of both of her breasts, I gave it to her every way our bodies could turn with me on top. I flipped her over onto her stomach and pushed her knees up until they were under her breasts and beat the pussy up like a drum. Karma started screaming in pleasurable pain and didn't stop until the girl occupying the next room banged on the wall, asking if she could join. We both laughed at the gesture. I slowed the beating down, but apparently, it was too slow for her.

"Let me sit on it, daddy. It's my turn to drive."

She moaned like something heard on one of those porno films as I went in deep and hard one last time before changing positions. I got on my back, and when she was secured in her new position of control, I licked and teased her nipples with my tongue. She took advantage of running the show and lifted my head off the bed, demanding that I suck on her breast. I didn't like the feeling of just lying there dead, so I began lifting my waist and stroking back. Karma's moans got deeper, until they turned into words.

"Grab my ass." I grabbed it, but not the way she wanted, and she had no problem correcting me. "Grab it harder! Squeeze my cheeks together and put all of it in me."

Her words mixed with her juices, which were now covering my lap and stomach, were too much for me to handle. The battle ended with us exploding simultaneously. I was upset that I couldn't last longer, but in all actuality, it wasn't minutes that had passed. It had been a couple of hours.

"Damn, girl, that was good shit."

"Jordan, I have something I need to tell you," she said lying next to me, rubbing on my chest.

~ ~ ~

Karma thought that it was time to tell him how he really got out of prison. It had been bugging her ever since she started falling for him. It probably wouldn't change his feelings, but she wanted him to know. Just as she was about to tell him, she received a text message. It was her sister.

DYNESHA: [sos]? ⚠ 🏠? 9

That was the code they used when something was wrong. It meant, "Come home ASAP." She jumped out of bed, but not too conspicuously.

~ ~ ~

"What's wrong?" I asked, noticing the sudden mood change.

"Nothing, I forgot I had to pick my sister up. She's mad at me," she lied. "I will be back after work to take you to your new job, sexy."

She bent down giving me the most seductive

kiss that I ever had, then headed out the door. I took a quick shower and lay down to get some rest. I was asleep as soon as my head hit the pillow.

Chapter Nine

It was a constant battle in the Valley View Projects, with cars pulling up, three or four at a time, in search of that almighty high. The young and older hustlers were scrambling to beat out the next man to get the sale. From a neighbor's perspective, it looked like a track meet. Whichever way you looked at it, they all had the same agenda: get that money. You could tell what type of fiends they were by the cars they drove. The ones that had a lot of money to spend would pull up in expensive nice cars, and others would be in average cars or walking to get high.

You still had to be on point, though, because looks could be deceiving. You had to always watch out for the undies that dressed as fiends, or you would find yourself sitting up in a cell in Gander Hill Prison, fighting for your life. This was some of the things that went on in Delaware, but none of that mattered right now. Jake needed to get some of the money back that those bitches robbed him for, so he could pay his connect back before the deadline. He didn't need those kind of problems right now. He already put word on the streets for any inform-ation of their whereabouts.

"You ready?"

"Let's do this shit," Hot Dog replied, loading one in the chamber of his gun.

BOOM!

The sound of Jake kicking the door off the hinges echoed through the house. Kareem jumped out of his seat as he saw the masked men enter with their guns drawn. The size of Jake's gun nearly made him piss his pants. Hot Dog had told Jake about this crib. All the hustlers were too busy getting money, so they didn't know what was going on at the stash house. Kareem was well respected in the projects. He had the south side sold up with dope and marijuana. Nobody fucked with him, because he had a bunch of young boys that weren't afraid to bust their guns for him. This was do or die right now, so Jake didn't care about any of that.

"Get the fuck on the floor," Jake yelled, waving his Desert Eagle.

Kareem got on his knees with his hands in

the air. Hot Dog had his weapon aimed at the three half-naked women sitting at the table, packaging up bundles of dope. None of the neighbors, nor any of the hustlers outside, heard the loud bang, which worked in Jake's favor. Hot Dog pushed the three women over to where Kareem was being held and made them get down on their knees next to him. Seeing the other masked man, he lowered his head in defeat.

"Where the fuck is the money at?" Jake demanded.

"Wha . . . wha . . . what money?" Kareem stuttered.

"Playing dumb gonna get one of you hurt," Jake stated, starting to get agitated, invading Kareem's personal space. He got so close to his face, he could smell the foul odor coming from his mouth. "I'm only asking one more time. Where. Is. The. Money?"

Before he could answer, Hot Dog smacked one of the females across the face with an open hand. She lay flat on her stomach, holding her cheek.

"Where is it?"

Without lifting his head, he pointed to the

refrigerator. Jake nodded to his man, and he walked over and opened the freezer. Inside were four neatly wrapped stacks of money.

"Bingo!" Hot Dog smiled.

They ordered all four hostages to lie flat on the floor, then hog-tied each of them. After making sure they were securely bound and gagged, they headed out the same way they came in, without being noticed. The whole stick-up took them about fifteen minutes.

"How much money is in there?" Hot Dog asked as they drove down Route 13, heading back to Wilmington.

"Not enough! This is only a portion of what was taken from me. They got everything, bro."

"Well I got some good news for you. I talked to some chick that goes to Del State, and she said she knows them."

"When was you going to tell me this shit? I need to find them bitches before they get comfortable. Where are they?"

"Chill, bro! She just hit me back while we were in that crib. She said they reside out PA."

"Where?" Jake said, getting angry.

"Somewhere out Scranton. She said they grew up together and if we needed to find them, that would be the place to start."

"How much did that cost you?"

"Nothing until we find them. I mean, I promised to take her out later, but that's about all," Hot Dog replied, shaking his head as if to say he really didn't want to.

"What's wrong with her?" Jake grinned.

"She's a big girl, dog."

"Big girls need love too! Handle your busy, bro."

"Whatever, man," he said, sucking his teeth.

"Anyway, looks like we're going to PA. First we have to stop by the block and tell Banger to hold shit down till we get back," Jake said as they headed toward Interstate 95.

~ ~ ~

Karma had me feeling like a new man. I stopped stressing over day-to-day existence and got on my shit. I was working twelve plus hours, four days a week at the club, trying to stack up enough bread to get my own apartment and car. She didn't complain, but I knew she was tired of having to drop me off and pick me up from work every day. She wanted me to stay with her instead of in that cheap-ass hotel I was in, but I just couldn't do it. I needed my own shit, not someone else's. I tried doing everything right, but it seemed like it wasn't enough for me. I needed more!

Since I've been home, I still haven't seen any of the people I used to roll with before I got booked. It didn't take long for that to change, working in a strip club. I was standing near the shampoo room when the last person I ever thought I would see, walked out. It wasn't until we locked eyes that reality sunk in. It was Abby, and she wasn't there alone. She was with the person I used to be cool with. Neither one of them moved or said a word until I said something to them.

"What's up?"

"Jordan, I didn't know you were home," Abby replied hesitantly.

She really didn't know if she should have stayed or made a run for the nearest exit. I really wasn't with the fake shit right now, so I got straight to the point.

"Yeah, I'm home. I don't care who you're fucking or about how you left me stinking in a prison cell 'cause you thought I would be there for a while. What I do care about is my fucking money that you took from me."

"Wait a minute, I didn't take shit fro—"

"Stop before another lie come out your mouth," I yelled over the music that was playing. Stizz stood there dumbfounded, listening to the conversation. He knew not to say shit because I would knock his teeth out. He wasn't no pussy, but he just couldn't fuck with me. You stole from me, and I want my shit back. Stizz, you were my man. I never expected you and Champ to leave me like that. Bitches come and go, but friends should be forever."

By this time, people were starting to stare, so I piped down. After all, I was at work and wasn't trying to get fired. I walked away leaving them wondering if I was going to smoke them or not when they left. In any other case, I probably would have, but this was not the time or place for it. You could tell they were both nervous as fuck as they walked out of the club, and kept looking back, making sure I didn't come out behind them. Abby wanted to tell me something, but never got the chance. I would find out later what she had to say.

"Who was that?" one of the bouncers came over and asked me.

"Nobody special!" I told him, not wanting to talk about it. He got the hint and walked off, making his rounds.

As I walked in the back room, one of the other bouncers was back there with one of the strippers. Cash had been working at the club for five years and had become the floor manager. I heard people always talking about how he was getting money outside of this place, but never said how.

What I saw them doing kind of froze me momentarily. Cash was positioned behind her, while she was filling her veins with a brown substance. His pants were down to his knees, and he was pounding her from the back. I knew the bouncers fucked the women in here, so it wasn't that much of a surprise. What surprised me was the fact that he let her shoot dope up out in the open. If the owner walked in on them, they both would be fired immediately. I stood by the door as a lookout until they were done.

Cash noticed what I was doing and gave me a head nod. Once he got his shit off, he motioned for me to come over.

"Come get some of this, J," he said, fixing his clothes.

"I'm good, bro."

"Suit yourself!"

I wasn't trying to fuck no dope fiend. I was more interested in where she was getting it. I waited for the girl to fix herself up and leave the room so I could ask him about it. I had an idea where it was coming from, but needed to be sure the rumors I'd been hearing around the club were true. In this establishment, women always talked about who the ballers were, and who was cheap. All most of them were really looking for was the day they would get out of this life and get pampered by one. I was thinking about getting back in the game, even if it was only temporary.

"Good looking on watching my back while I was handling business," Cash said, giving me a fist bump. "I know I was fucking up by letting her do that shit, but the pussy was good."

Even in his work uniform, you could see that he was getting money. The expensive watch and glasses he wore proved it. Being jealous was for a fool, and I was far from foolish. I looked him dead in the eyes and kept it real.

"However you're getting your money, I want in. I've lost a lot since I was gone, and I'm trying to get it back!"

"I don't know what you're talking about. I work hard every day to get this money. Keep working hard and you will get where I'm at."

"Naw. I'm talking about—"

Cash put his index finger up in the air as if to shut me up, because a couple of girls had entered the locker room. He hurriedly grabbed his radio off the table and walked past me.

"Let's get back to work, youngster."

The arrogant muthafucka brushed me off without trying to hear me out. He was acting like he was above me or something, which would usually make niggas like me find a way to sit his ass down. Luckily for me, I was trying to leave that life in the past. Instead of plotting to kill him, though, I decided to make it my business to go the opposite way whenever he was around, because the urge to check the nigga would cost me my parole and my new boo.

Because of the line of work we were in, eventually we had to work together. We were having a chocolate syrup pool fight, so we all had to be up on stage with the women. Me and Cash were in charge of making sure none of the them got hurt, and wiping the chocolate off their naked bodies afterward. Boy, were there some stacked bitches working up in that joint!

"So if you don't mind me asking, why do you need money so bad that you are willing to sacrifice your freedom?" Cash asked, trying to spark a conversation after we closed and were cleaning up. "It gotta be for something big."

"Yeah, it is." I fought myself about telling this nigga anything, then said fuck it. "I'm tired of living in a dirty-ass hotel. I need my own spot."

He looked uneasy about my response, like he didn't know what to say. He continued taking the candles off the table, smirking the whole time. I took that as a sign of disrespect.

"Man, fuck this shit," I said, walking away, until I felt his hand on my shoulder, stopping me. "What?" I snapped, eye-checking the shit out of his hand to let him know he shouldn't have touched me.

"You need to learn how to control them emotions," Cash said, shaking his head. "If you want to get at the money, fix that attitude."

He handed me a business card that didn't have a name or any of the other information business cards usually have. The only thing on the card was a printed telephone number in a bold font.

"Give me a call. I might have a sales position for you."

"A sales position? What we selling?" I asked, waiting for an answer.

"You ain't selling shit. Not yet, that is. It's a process, that takes some time, learning, and the right attitude. We will talk more about it later."

"Whatever," I said, losing interest and heading up to the office to clock out, because I knew Karma was outside waiting on me. He waited by the exit door for me until I grabbed my stuff to leave. As I walked out the door and headed for the passenger side of the car, he yelled out to me.

"Jordan, what do you know about the dope game?"

Immediately, all my interest returned. He was now talking my language, and from that point on, I knew that I would be back to where I left off in no time . . .

Chapter Ten

I hated to lie to Karma, but if she knew I was meeting up with Cash over some drugs, she would take it as regression. I had made so many positive strides at securing my future that she wouldn't understand why I'd be willing to risk it all for greed. Truth is, I wasn't in it for greed, I was just trying to get back by any means necessary. I fed her a line of bullshit about us having to renovate one part of the club for an upcoming event and asked if I could use her car.

"I don't want you dropping me off today, baby. I don't know how long we will be, and if it's only a couple of hours, we can chill in bed for the rest of the day, if you know what I mean," I told her, rubbing her pussy under the sheet.

"What if you have to be there all day and I'm stuck here stranded, doing nothing. I'll just drop you off, and you can call me when you're ready. I have to go see my sisters anyway."

"Why can't they just come pick you up?"

"Hell no, Jordan!"

Nothing I said would get her to throw me her

keys, because her real problem with me using her car was that I didn't have my license back yet. She let me drive while she was in the passenger seat, but that was as far as it went until my year suspension was up. I didn't want to argue with her about it. She just gave me all the confirmation I needed to hurry up and get money so I could get my own shit.

I had her drop me off at work, then called an Uber to take me to the restaurant at the Wyoming Valley Mall where we were supposed to meet up. Cash was waiting for me when I walked in. I didn't even get a chance to sit down and taste any of the food.

"Let's take a walk through the mall and talk," he said, dropping some money on the table for the food he just ate. I picked up a couple of pieces of turkey bacon from the plate and followed him out. "So tell me what you know about the dope game, Jordan?"

"Before I went to prison, I had Scranton on lock with dope. I don't know when you stepped onto the scene, but this was me," I began, waving my hands in the air. "Now I come home and the people I thought was my friends, took over and left me high and dry. I'm not worried, though, because what goes around, comes around, and I don't forget."

"To answer your question, I moved out here in Wilkes-Barre about two years ago. I think I may have the best supplier in the city. My product comes pure and uncut. You have to handle this shit carefully or you'll get addicted. If you're too scared to get back in this business, I understand, and there will be no hard feelings. My motto is, scared money don't make no money. I can't fuck with you, Jordan, if you're scared. A scared nigga will have me sitting behind bars."

"I ain't scared. I wouldn't be here if I was," I blurted out. "If you think I'm one of those scared niggas, then you don't know me at all, and better do your research on me. I shouldn't have to work for nobody, when I had my own shit before I went away. I plan on paying some people a visit, but I'll do that on my time."

"That right there brings me to my next lesson. You have to learn to respect the hand that feeds you. Trust me, I get it! You're big, bad-ass Jordan, who feels like he has to prove something to the world after the shit that those fuck boys did to you when you were down. I promise you that you'll never get a bite off my plate, or even the chance to lick the fucking plate clean unless you fix that attitude."

If this was a few years ago, Cash would be lying in a pool of his own blood after the way he just talked to me. But right now he was the connection I needed, so I had to bite my tongue. It's amazing how fast a nigga can go from having everything, to nothing. That was my situation right now, and I needed to make it better before I could do what I wanted. In a matter of time, I would make him regret talking to me in that tone.

"We're done for the day," Cash said.

He started walking back in the direction of the restaurant, but I didn't move. When he noticed I wasn't following him, he turned and came back, like he was ready to talk shit. I was tired of his shit at this point. I wasn't one of those young bulls he had working for him. Before he could open his mouth to say anything to me, I spoke up.

"We're not done for the day. You had something planned for me, and I want to know what it is. I respect you and what you were saying. Respect is everything, but it goes both ways. I understand I'm an invited guest to your world, but I can only give the amount of respect I'm getting in return. As long as you remember that I'm a man and you talk to me like one, this shit will ride smoother than your Maybach."

"Finally, we are getting somewhere, and done, Jordan!" Cash smirked.

We went back to the restaurant and sat and talked for hours. He ran down his whole operation to me and told me that I would be his right-hand man. He told me how he had fucked with another coworker at the club and it backfired on him. He got greedy with the shit and ended up being carried out in handcuffs. Even though he never snitched, and took the charge like a man, Cash was skeptical of who he trusted. Before we went our separate ways, he handed me a cellphone.

"This is a business-related phone only. Nobody should have this number unless I give it to them or we both agree to it. Business and personal shit never work out, so don't be tempted to mix the two. When this phone rings, be ready to roll out. What are you driving around in, anyway?"

I explained my situation, and we went

straight to a used car lot. Two hours later, I pulled up to Karma's crib in my used Mazda CX9 that Cash had purchased for me. Since I was working now, he told me that I might be able to get my license reinstated early, on some work permit shit. I decided I would go this weekend to take care of it.

Karma wasn't home when I got there, so I used the spare key she gave me to let myself in. I tried to call her and let her know I was there, since this was my first time in her crib without her, but her cell kept going straight to voicemail. I sat on the couch and watched TV for an hour, then boredom kicked in. I began working out until I was covered in sweat. I was lying there on the carpet next to the bed, about to take a nap, but something under the bed caught my eye. There was a large briefcase sitting there. The first thing I thought about as I pulled it out was that she was hiding some freaky sex toys in it.

I opened it up and got the surprise of a lifetime. The briefcase was full of money, jewelry, and other expensive items. The cash was neatly wrapped in rubber bands. There was so much, I couldn't even count it without taking it out of the briefcase. Where did she get all this money, and why was it hiding under her bed? I was looking over the expensive jewelry, when I spotted some newspaper clippings and transcripts. Upon further inspection, it was clippings of me and my case. With the transcripts was a motion to reduce the sentence that was imposed on me by my judge. I was shocked to see this. Did she have something to do with me getting released early? Just as I was about to flip the fourth page, I heard someone putting a key in the keyhole. Karma came in and threw her bags down onto the dining room table.

"Shit!" I whispered, closing the briefcase and sliding it back under the bed just in time.

She almost caught me as she walked in the room, but I pretended to do pushups. I kind of startled her when she spotted me.

"How did you get home?" she asked, kicking off her shoes.

I didn't respond because I didn't want to tell her about the car yet. I pulled her down on my lap and gave her a peck on the lips. That did the trick, because she didn't ask me again about how I got there. She put her arms around my neck and smiled.

"I got you something!"

"What?" I replied, looking into her eyes.

"After I met up with my sisters, I stopped by the store and grabbed you a couple of things," Karma said, getting off my lap. She grabbed a bag that contained a shoe box and handed to me. "Open it!"

She wore an excited look on her face as I released the drawstring on the bag. Karma had brought me a fresh pair of Jordans. I couldn't pretend like I wasn't excited. She had bent over backward to make me happy, and I loved her for it.

"Here. Go get your musty ass in the shower and put on some of that cologne I got you. I want some eye candy to look at while I eat." She smirked.

I wanted to talk to her about what was under her bed, but I didn't want her to know that I had been snooping around while she was gone. I got in the shower, shaved, and washed up. I threw on a black wifebeater and a new pair of boxer briefs I had sitting in my overnight bag that I kept there when I stayed the night, then got dressed. I sprayed some of the cologne on and checked myself in the mirror. I felt like new money for once, since being home. When I walked into the living room to model my shit for Karma, she had a fucked-up look on her face.

"Jordan, whose cellphone is this? I thought you said you weren't going to get one until I added you to my plan."

The phone had been in my jacket pocket, which meant she had gone snooping through my shit, or it had rung and had caught her attention. I snatched the phone out of her hand, and there were two missed calls displayed on the screen. Without hesitation, I called the number back.

"Where you at, Jay? You ready to make a move with me?"

"Hell yeah. Where are we meeting at?" I replied. I could tell Cash was driving his car, because I could hear traffic in the background.

"On my way to your hotel. I'll be pulling up in about ten minutes to get you. Be outside."

"I'm at my girl's spot, but I'll be there in fifteen."

"Where the fuck do you think you're going?" Karma snapped as soon as I ended the call and threw my jacket on. "We're supposed to be going out to eat, and who the fuck was that calling you, Jordan?"

I couldn't tell her the truth, and I didn't have enough time to come up with a lie to smooth shit over. Besides, we were both living a lie, I thought to myself, looking toward the bed, but what kind of lie was she living? Right now, I needed to bounce.

"A friend from work, and we will go out to eat when I get back, babe," I said, leaning in to kiss her on the cheek, but she stepped back.

"You think I'm dumb, don't you? I graduated from law school, Jordan. I'm a fucking lawyer! All of a sudden you have friends and a cellphone that I don't even have the number to, but they do. You work at a strip club. So who is she? Tell that bitch you're on the way to give her that shit back, and I'm taking you to do it."

Karma grabbed her car keys off the table and started putting on her shoes. I knew this wasn't the time to tell her about the car, but I pulled out my keys, hoping she'd catch on.

"There ain't no bitch, Karma! I keep telling your insecure ass that it's all about you. I'm about to meet up with my boy from work for a second, and then I'll be back to pick you up. Plus we need to have a conversation about what's under your bed," I said sarcastically to get the attention off of me. "Go get ready."

"What, you were going through my shit?" she asked.

I didn't answer her and opened the door to leave. A half-full soda bottle that she had been drinking when she came in, came flying over my head.

"You have the bitch picking you up from my house? Oh, hell naw. I don't know who you think you fucking with, but both of y'all will be dead if she's out there waiting on you!"

Karma ran to the closet and grabbed a bat. I took off running, with her right behind me. I jumped in my car, and threw it in reverse before she came outside.

"I love you, baby. I'll be right back," I told her, rolling my window down.

Karma said a lot of fucked-up shit in those couple of seconds, but the only words I was able to make out were, "And you got a car! Fuck you and that bitch, Jordan. I'm done with you!"

I hit a few blocks to make sure she hadn't followed me in her car, then pulled out my phone and called Cash back.

"Change of plans. Can you pick me up from the Steamtown Mall parking lot? My girl was just tripping, and I don't want to leave my car where she can get to it."

Cash laughed and then said, "Aw, you got you one of those types. I'll be there in a couple of minutes."

When I pulled up, I parked and waited. After ten minutes, I looked around for Cash's car, but didn't see it. He called me as I was picking up the phone to call him.

"Turn around. That's me in the black Ford F150."

I looked in my rearview mirror and spotted him parking behind me. I hopped out of my car, and into the passenger side of his.

"What's up with your shorty? You didn't tell her about our business arrangement, did you?" he asked with concern in his voice.

"No. That's why she's tripping. I came home with a phone and a car, so now she's questioning me about an invisible bitch, but I didn't answer. Next thing I know, she's throwing soda bottles at me and chasing me out of the house swinging a baseball bat."

"Do you love her, or is she just a throwaway piece?" Cash asked. He died laughing as he pulled out of the parking garage.

"Naw, I love her and tried to tell that to her crazy ass as I was peeling off, but she wasn't trying to hear that shit."

"How long have y'all been kicking it?"

"Not long! She's wife material, but she got some secrets that we need to get to the bottom of before we can move forward in our relationship." I was still thinking about that shit in the briefcase. Was she some kind of jewel smuggler, or doing some illegal shit?

"So peep this. If she got secrets, then you do too! Y'all haven't been together long enough or built enough trust, from what it sounds like, for you to be spilling your guts about what you're getting into. She may be riding with you now, but you don't know how well she'll have your back if something pops off and the police have to question her."

"See, that's the thing, we kind of knew each other since we were in high school. We just only really spoke one time," I said, thinking about the club.

"That's still not fully knowing each other, bro." Cash reached into his glove box and retrieved another phone that was identical to the one he gave me. "This will be your personal line.

Your girl won't know that this ain't the same phone she saw you with earlier. My number is the only one stored in there. Give her the number to help calm her ass down some. When you're around her, keep your business phone somewhere safe. You can even forward these calls to that one. You can't have any missed calls, because that will mean missed money. You have been saving bread, right?"

"Yeah, but it's only around $750 dollars, because I'm paying $40 a day for the hotel room."

"Okay, so tell her you took your first three paychecks to cop the car. Wait. She don't have access to your money, do she?"

"Naw. I keep my money on this prepaid debit card," I said, pulling out my Green Dot money card.

"That's the money from working at the club?"

"Yup, and all my tips too!"

"Okay, get yourself a bank account, then set up direct deposit so the money from work goes straight into that account. You can use your prepaid card for the money you make with me. We will make eighty or better, depending on the customer, off of a bundle. Money will be coming your way fast, so start thinking of hiding places," Cash joked.

We headed out Olyphant PA to meet a potential buyer. The whole time, my mind was on Karma. I text her, but she didn't reply. Then it came.

"What do you want?" Right after she texted back, she started blowing my phone up with call after call, but I sent her to voicemail every time.

Then I sent her another text: "Text me, baby. I can't talk right now."

Karma didn't waste any time getting shit off her chest once she read my message. She started sending these extra-long-ass texts, asking me where I got the car and phone from, talking shit about if I was fucking with another bitch, she was going to kill me, and how if I was with the bitch when she found me, we both would be dead.

I responded back with the story that me and Cash had just discussed. I told her that the phone was my surprise to her, because I couldn't reach her when I left work, and that everything I was doing was to better us. I could tell she was calming down, because her next text finally indicated that she had heard what I had been saying to her.

"Do you really ♥me, babe? If so, why did you say it for the first time when you were driving off?"

"I didn't want to get hit with a baseball bat. 😅? Lol."

"I ♡ you too. Are you on your way back? I'm hungry and missing you."

"No. Grab something, baby, and I'll see you when I get back. I'm going to be longer than I thought."

"Fuck you, Jordan! Don't come back. Go to your shithole hotel room tonight. I'm going out."

I started to ask where she was going, who she was going with, and when she was coming back, but I let it go and just responded, "👍 No problem, I will sleep in my room tonight. Don't be out there doing shit that's gonna get somebody fucked up. I 💓 you."

I tucked my phone in my pocket so I could focus on the business at hand. I couldn't worry about her or her attitude right now. I would deal with that some other time. Nothing would fuck this up for me.

Chapter Eleven

Kildare's Irish Pub, a popular bar and lounge located across the street from the Hilton where Jake and Hot Dog had been staying, was where all the college students and club hoppers went if they weren't at Levels, to have a good time. Hot Dog pulled into the small lot and parked close to the door, just in case they needed to make a fast exit. They could have walked across the street, but there was a reason they didn't: they needed to keep their weapons close.

"Let's see what this joint is hitting for since we out here," he said to Jake as they stepped out of the car.

"We came out here on business, not to burn the money we got from the lick nigga," Jake said reluctantly.

"Trust me, I know why we're here. But for tonight, let's fuck some of these Scranton bitches. Look at all that ass right there," Hot Dog said, pointing to this thick female walking in the door with two of her friends right behind her.

Jake looked at the girls and surrendered to

the thought of getting his dick wet tonight. Hot Dog was always the one that wanted to make good out of a bad situation, but it wasn't his neck on the line. Jake knew that if anything popped off, though, he would have his back, and vice versa.

"Cool, let's grab some skins to take back to the telly with us," Jake replied.

Once inside the bar, they headed straight to the bar and ordered drinks. The bartender passed them their drinks and was given a very generous tip by Hot Dog. It was mad crowded in there with people dancing and having a good time. After getting a couple of drinks in his system, Jake was in full flirt mode. He searched the crowd, looking for the thick chick they saw earlier. She was in the middle of the floor dancing with one of the girls she came with.

"I'll be back," he leaned over and told his homie. "I'm about to holla at shorty and see what she getting into."

"See what's up with her friend too," Hot Dog yelled out.

He ordered another drink from the bad-ass bartender, then scooped his surroundings checking out all the bad chicks that was there.

His eyes stopped on two beautiful women that were just clearing security and stepping into the building. They walked over and sat in the two stools next to him. He stared seductively at the beauties as if they were a piece of candy that he wanted to eat up.

"Which one of y'all know how to roll?" Hot Dog asked, holding up the bag of marijuana and a Game.

That got the women's attention, causing them to stop what they were doing and look at him. One of the women held out her hand.

"Here, I'll roll that shit," one girl said, grabbing the weed and cigar from him.

"Damn, okay! Here you go, sexy," Hot Dog said, holding his hand up in a surrendering position. "By the way , my name is Hot Dog, but you can call me Dog. What's y'all names?"

"My name is Heaven, and her name is Ashley," she replied as they stepped outside to smoke.

After blowing, they came back in, and Hot Dog brought them drinks. He was holding a conversation with Heaven, when Jake walked back up and started going at Ashley. He figured that he wasn't getting anywhere with the other chicks because they were acting as if they were loyal to their men. She told him that she had a boyfriend that didn't like doing shit but sitting in the house playing video games with his boys. Jake laughed because whenever he wasn't putting in work, he liked playing PlayStation, or Xbox too.

Four apple martinis apiece later, the music was beginning to sound extra good to the women. Heaven started moved in her seat.

"That's my shit," Ashley said, bobbing her head to Tory Lanez's "On My Level 2."

"So what's up with you, sexy? You trying to dance for a minute?" Hot Dog asked, standing up.

"Yeah, we can do that," Heaven said, and looked back at her girl with a smile and a wink.

Jake and Ashley stayed at the bar drinking shot after shot, not really feeling their surroundings, while their friends did their thing on the dance floor. This was only her fourth time ever coming to this club. Usually, she would be at Levels with the rest of her college friends. A couple of their friends wanted to come here first though, so she did.

"Look at this nigga! He swear he can dance,"

Jake said, watching Hot Dog do some dumb-ass dance as the girl shook her ass all over him.

"Mmm-hmm, they might as well be fucking the way she giving it back," Ashley said as Heaven threw her leg around Hot Dog's waist.

By this time, two more girls had come over to where Ashley and Jake were sitting. It was the same girls that he had been talking to earlier. He didn't know they were together, or even knew each other. He hoped they didn't try to throw salt on his game. To his surprise, they didn't.

"We're ready to leave this joint and go to the after hour," one of them said.

"Well, it was nice talking to you, Jake, but I have to bounce," she told him as they walked over toward Heaven. Jake shook his head and ordered another drink from the bartender.

Once they made their way through the crowd, one of the girls yelled over the music and told Heaven that they were ready to leave. She turned to her new friend and broke the news of her early departure as easily as possible. She knew he'd be upset because he'd been talking slick all night, plus she felt how big his package was while her leg was on his waist.

"Look, I'm about to bounce because my girls are ready to leave," she said.

"Huh? So you are going to leave me just like that?" he asked. "I thought we were going to chill and get to know each other. Damn, tell them that I got you. I'll make sure you get home safely."

"I don't even know you like that. You could be a serial killer," she joked.

"Do I look like a serial killer?" he asked, stepping back some.

"I don't know," Heaven said cautiously.

"Come on, girl, what you going to do?" Ashley said, irritated.

Heaven looked at them, then back at Hot Dog, who was standing there giving her the puppy-eyed look, which made her smile.

"I'm a chill here. Dog is going to bring me home."

"You is a stupid bitch!" Mia said, and spun on her heels in disgust. "Come on, y'all."

Heaven felt the sting of her friend's words but let them bounce off. They all had men to go home to, plus they were straight. She had no one and was working all kinds of hours, living from paycheck to paycheck, because nobody was giving her shit. Hot Dog looked like he was getting money, and she wanted a piece of the pie.

"You straight?" he asked.

"Yeah, I'm straight."

~ ~ ~

Hot Dog held Heaven's arm as she staggered away from Kildare's, and led her over to his car. Jake stayed there for a while, trying to pick something else up. Since they were only across the street from the hotel room, he told Hot Dog to take the car with him. Heaven was mad at herself for allowing herself to get so high and couldn't shake off the intoxicants. She was conscious and knew what was going on, but she felt as if she was moving in slow motion.

"Where would you like to go?" Hot Dog asked.

"I don't know. You're the one driving, right? I'm trying to figure out why we're still sitting here," she replied, and laid her seat all the way back.

"My hotel is right across the street, if you trying to go there."

She nodded her head. " Let's go then!"

Hot Dog parked in the empty space, and

they stepped out of the car. He led her through the front doors and to the elevator. When they reached the tenth floor, Hot Dog slid the credit card-type key into the door and waited for the green light, before turning the knob. He held the door open for Heaven and she entered the plush room.

"I'm going to the bathroom," Hot Dog said as Heaven opened the drapes to look out at the view of Scranton.

She turned to look at how big the room was. It had a huge entertainment center and soft leather furniture, with a queen-size bed that was placed against the wall in front of the huge window. Hot Dog came out dressed in only his boxers.

"I'm getting in the Jacuzzi. Are you going to join me?" Heaven nodded her head yes, then sat her purse down on the bed.

Hot Dog got in and lay back, sipping on some liquor, while he watched Heaven undress. She came out of her clothes piece by piece as provocatively as she could, revealing her beautiful caramel skin. When she stood before him in her red thong and matching strapless bra, he could only shake his head.

"What's wrong?" she asked as he stared at her oddly. The way her body looked as she stood there half naked made his dick come to life and stand at attention. It took him a couple more minutes before he could speak.

"Yo, anybody ever tell you how good you look?"

"I've heard it before," she said, and stepped into the Jacuzzi.

Heaven sat back against the other wall of the Jacuzzi and faced Hot Dog while he poured her a drink. She let her arms spread out, resting over the base of the Jacuzzi, and arched her back, pushing her titties up. Using her foot, she slid it under the water and placed it on his dick and wiggled her toes, causing him to almost spill his drink.

"You alright?" she teased.

"Don't start nothing you can't finish," he said.

"I thought you'd never ask," she said, sliding across the Jacuzzi and sitting on his lap.

Heaven wrapped her legs around his waist and her arms around his neck, then kissed him on the forehead, then the lips. The two of them teased each other with foreplay for about twenty minutes. Then, just like that, Hot Dog stood up with Heaven still wrapped around his body, squeezing her ass, and walked over to the bed. "You have a rubber?" Heaven asked as he laid her down on the bed. "No glove, no love!" "Yeah, I got one," he replied, walking away to retrieve it from his pants pocket. When he came back, Heaven was lying on top of the bed butt naked. Instantly seeing this beautiful dime piece lying on the bed had his dick rock hard. He quickly stepped out of his boxers and slid the extra-sensitive Magnum on.

"Take your time, I haven't done it in a while," she lied as Hot Dog climbed on top of her. Heaven reached down and grabbed his mans, then guided him into her moist hole. Hot Dog started off at first with a smooth stroke as Heaven held one of her legs up in the air, grinding her hips in a circular motion.

"Sssssssss, damn, baby!" Hot Dog squealed. "This pussy is blazing."

"Is it? Tell me it's good again. Tell me my pussy is good again!" she moaned.

"It's good, baby! This pussy is so fucking good," Hot Dog said as Heaven flipped him over and straddled his pelvic area.

"Let me ride it, baby." Just like that, Heaven

snapped, letting her freaky side come out to play. She placed both of her hands on his chest, raising her body, then flopped down, grinding and twisting until she felt him melt inside her. "Damn, you came already?"

He didn't even have to answer because the look of shame was written all over his face. She reached down and grabbed his dick again to make sure the rubber stayed on when she got up.

"Don't feel bad, you said it was blazing. You're not the first, and probably won't be the last one-minute man I fuck. If you can get it back up again in the next few minutes, we can go again."

~ ~ ~

"You trying to get out of here?" Jake asked some chick he just bought three drinks for.

"Sure, but I can't stay out all night because I have a son at home. Where we going?" the female asked, standing up.

"Hold on!" Jake had to take a second look at the person he saw walking in his direction. Subconsciously, he reached to his waist for his gun, but realized that it wasn't there.

"What's wrong?" the female asked, seeing the change in his demeanor.

"There that bitch go right there," he mumbled to himself.

"Who you talking to?"

Just as he was about to respond, he and Dynesha locked eyes. If looks could kill, they both would be dead right now. Jake stood there, thinking of his next move, when Dynesha reached inside her purse and pulled out her gun. Jake didn't know what to do. He wondered how the fuck she was able to get her shit in and he couldn't. She started walking toward him.

Jake looked around, trying to figure out a way out of there. That's when he noticed the doors to the outside balcony. He rushed through the crowd, with the Dynesha on his heels. He reached for his phone and tried to call Hot Dog, but he didn't answer.

"Fuck," he yelled out, running through the parking lot, trying to get to the hotel.

Dynesha came out of the bar, firing four shots in his direction. Jake was able to dodge three of them, but the fourth one hit him in the shoulder, knocking him to the ground. Adrenaline kicked in, and he jumped to his feet, running across the street. By now, pedestrians were scattering to get out of the way. Dynesha continued firing at Jake, catching him in the leg. He made it inside the lobby of the hotel, before collapsing on the lobby floor. Dynesha jumped in her car and sped away. What he didn't know was, if Dynesha wanted to kill him, she could have easily done so. She was a marksman and was very accurate. Scranton police flooded the area and rushed Jake to Geisinger Hospital.

The whole time all that commotion was going on downstairs, Hot Dog was too busy trying to bust a nut. He never knew his partner had gotten shot. All hell was about to break loose in Lackawanna County.

Chapter Twelve

I was spending so much time in the streets, that I was neglecting what was important to me. I let the money blind me. It was coming in so rapidly that I had to start using my regular bank account instead of the prepaid, because it could only hold so much. Ever since my fallout with Karma, I hadn't spoken with her. There were times when I wanted to slide up on her, but my pride got the best of me. I didn't want no chick to ever see me sweating them. That was just something I don't do.

It was Cash's birthday, so me, him, and his brother headed out to Philly to celebrate. Vanity Grand's line was packed outside, but we walked straight to the front. The first fifty or so people in line were nothing but beautiful women.

"What's up Cash Money? Go right on in," the bouncer said, giving him a half hug.

The dance floor was packed as we headed over to the VIP area. It took us twenty minutes just to get seated on one of the leather couches due to everybody wanting to shake Cash's hand. I didn't know he was such a celebrity everywhere, especially in Philly. I was getting shown love like I had been with them for years. It felt good. Every five minutes, I could hear bottles popping and niggas making toasts on behalf of Cash.

"Damn, nigga, they showing you love like you from here," I said after all the birthday wishes slowed down some.

"It ain't shit, Jay. I was born and raised in Philly. After I came home in 2016 from my state bid, I wanted to get out of the city, so I moved out Scranton. This party is going to be off-the-wall crazy. Make sure you enjoy yourself."

Cash got up to greet some more of his newly arrived guests, while his brother, Trevor, slid down on the couch next to me.

"Come take a walk with me," he said.

When he stood to his feet, so did I. Cash was talking to some guests when we walked by him, but kept his eyes on us.

"Here," Trevor said as soon as we entered the men's bathroom. He lifted up the back of his shirt and handed me a gun. "Just in case something pops off because my brother is back in town."

I hadn't touched a gun since that incident at the Red Roof Inn, so to be holding a weapon in my hand again made me feel uneasy. What if I got arrested out here? My PO would drop a detainer on me so quick. I wasn't even supposed to be out here without letting him know. Fuck it, it was too late to be contemplating options now.

"Is he beefing with somebody?" I asked, thinking that was the reason he really left Philadelphia, but Trevor immediately erased that theory.

"Naw. Cash don't do no beefs, but all these smiling faces ain't as genuine as they seem. Philly niggas are jealous, cold-hearted, grimy individuals. I'm giving you this just in case."

I put the gun on my waist, but still felt kind of nervous holding a weapon again. As I was covering the handle with my shirt, a couple of niggas walked in to use the bathroom. They nodded in our direction, then walked toward the urinals.

"Let's go dance with some of Philly's finest."

The dance floor was even more crowded than before. It seemed like every female I laid my eyes on was prettier than the other. Even the big girls in here had sex appeal and could get it. I'd never been with a big girl before, but, damn. I danced from one cutie to the next, making my way around the room. Trevor kept offering me drinks or inviting me to come back up to VIP and get fucked up with them, but I was straight. Someone needed to be on point in case something popped off.

I danced until my knees started hurting. I finally made my way back up to VIP to sit down, but it was blocked off and two security officers were standing there.

"Hold on for a minute; the birthday boy is getting his birthday present," one of the huge men said.

"Yo, that's my man. Let him through. Jay, get your ass up here." Cash smirked.

"Have fun." The bouncer smiled, moving to the side.

Soon as I made my way over to Cash, all I could see was him sitting on the couch, smoking a dutch with one hand and sipping on something dark with the other. His boxers and pants were at his ankles. There were two bitches, one black and the other white, on their knees in front of him, fighting over whose mouth his dick would go in next, and there were two more chicks standing there watching, waiting their turns.

"Trevor is wild for this one. Two sets of head-hunting identical twins. Have a seat and help me unwrap my gifts."

"Naw, dawg, that's all you. Enjoy your present."

"Damn, Jay. That little chick got you bugging. We came here to have fun, nigga. Well, you can at least hit this dutch with me, or did she say you can't smoke either?" Cash said sarcastically, holding the dutch up in front of me.

I sat on the far end of the couch, turned my back to him, and reached for the dutch. After two puffs of the loud, I was high as fuck. I pulled out my phone and called Karma, but she wasn't answering. Instead, she sent me a text message back.

Karma: "I'm busy. I'll be by there to see you tomorrow! bye! ✋."

Busy? I started blowing up her phone, and every time she forward me to her voicemail and then turned her phone off.

"Fuck it. If she wants to play games, so will I," I mumbled to myself.

The weed had let Cash's words not to trust a

bitch take dominance over my thoughts. I hit the dutch a few more times, then asked Trevor to get me a cup of whatever it was that Cash was drinking.

"That's what the fuck I'm talking about, Jay. She probably out there fucking off anyway. You might as well be doing the same."

Trevor came back with my glass of Hennessey, and it was on. I didn't penetrate none of the bad females, because I had pussy at home, but I damn sure killed their throats. I had both chicks leaving with my unborn kids floating around their digestive systems.

"You good, Jay?" Cash asked, sipping the Henny.

"I'm straight," I replied. Guilt started kicking in as my high started coming down, but it was too late to press the rewind button now. I'd just have to treat Philly like Vegas and let whatever happened here, stay here.

We left the club around four without anything popping off. We sobered up at Penrose Dinner in South Philly while we ate. After breakfast, we jumped on Interstate 95, heading home. I fell asleep as soon as we got in the car, and when Cash woke me up a little over two hours later, we were back in Scranton at my car.

"Get you a few hours of sleep, Jay. Then we back at it. There's money to be made."

I headed straight to my hotel room to get some rest. I never thought about it until now, but I should have been more wise about where I was staying. I was actually staying in the hotel where we killed somebody. "Fuck it," I thought to myself, walking into my room. I jumped in bed fully dressed and passed the fuck out. I woke up at around one in the afternoon to Mr. Jamison ringing my phone. He was calling to see if I was still coming over to eat. Even though I was working and doing my thing on the side, I still tried to meet them every Sunday for dinner, before I had to go to the club. They still were like family to me.

"I'll be there in thirty minutes. Let me jump in the shower and throw some clothes on," I told him after talking for a couple of minutes.

I turned the shower water on cold, and it gave me life. When I pulled up to the house, Karma's car was parked in the driveway. I had tried to call her when I got out of the shower, but her phone had still been going straight to voicemail. I walked in the house and greeted

Mrs. Jamison with a kiss on the cheek, then sat down at the table. For some reason today seemed different. Normally, Karma sat next to me at the table. This time, she was sitting in between the Jamisons, and this was the first dinner we ate in complete silence.

I didn't know what she had told her family about the night before, but the Jamisons were keeping their words short and dry. I didn't realize until I reached across the table to grab another dinner roll, that Karma was rocking a hickey the size of a quarter on her neck.

"What the fuck is that?" I asked.

Everyone looked up from their plates except for Karma. She continued to eat, pretending she didn't know who I was talking to. The first thing that came to mind was that she was tired of fucking with a broke-ass nigga like me and had gone back to her rich boyfriend.

"Karma!"

She looked at me when I called her name, and said, "What, Jordan?"

"What the fuck is that on the side of your neck?"

Mrs. Jamison said something about having a sweet potato pie in the oven and got up, and Mr.

Jamison volunteered to help her with it. I waited for the them to leave the room before I stood up to take a closer look at her neck. As I stared at it, I noticed Karma had a slight smile on her face.

"Oh, you think this shit is funny, huh?"

"I don't know what you're talking about, Jordan, but did you have fun with your new friend last night?"

"You know exactly what I'm talking about. I'm talking about that hickey you got on your fucking neck," I snapped. She was playing games with me . That was why her ass had decided to wear that strapless top, to throw the shit in my face. "What the fuck did you do last night, or should I say, who did you do?"

"Fuck you, Jordan. Don't question me until you've checked yourself first!"

We went back and forth about it, screaming and yelling until Mr. Jamison came back in the room, handed me a Styrofoam plate of food, and asked me to leave. That was the first time since Abby that my heart felt like it had been shredded to pieces. I jumped in my car and peeled off, with no regard for anybody or anything.

"Fuck her. Karma is a bitch!"

Chapter Thirteen

"The nigga was at Kildare's," **Dynesha said,**
talking to her sisters on a group video chat.
"How the hell did he find out where we
were?" Rynesha replied in a worried tone. "We
should have bodied that nigga when we were in
that hotel room."

"That really doesn't matter right now. I had
the chance last night, but I let the nigga breathe.
I gave him a shoulder and leg shot, hoping that
he gets the message and goes back to
Delaware."

"Stop talking like that on here, Dy," Rynesha
said, realizing how reckless they had been
talking. "You know them people can hear
everything. Karma, why you looking all sad and
shit. Did that nigga do something to you, 'cause
we can pay his ass a visit and talk some sense
into him?"

"No, leave him alone," she said with a
concerned look on her face. "He didn't do
anything to me. I have to see how much the
police know about what happened. I wish you

would have called me as soon as it happened, so we could have prepared just in case the cops come looking. I told you before that I can't keep protecting y'all if I'm left in the dark."

"What do you mean? Once again, we're telling you now," Dynesha snapped.

"Dy, I don't give a damn about your attitude. I'm tired of your shit anyway, and y'all need to come get that shit you left at my crib before he finds it." Little did Karma know, her worst fears had already come true. "How the fuck am I supposed to explain that?"

"Stop acting like a bitch, Karma. He shouldn't be going through your shit anyway."

"And you shouldn't be such a fucking thief," Karma shot back.

"Fuck you, bitch. Ry, I will see you later. I'm tired of talking to her whipped ass. She don't have to worry about me asking for her help anymore. If anything happens, I'll figure it out my fucking self.

" Dy, don't be that way," Rynesha said, trying to calm the situation down before it got worse.

"Fuck her, I'm out," Dynesha said, disconnecting from their video chat.

All the arguing with her sister, and the chain

of events that happened outside of Kildare's, had her stressed out. She needed to relieve some of the tension she was feeling, and she knew exactly how to do so. She went up to her bedroom and took off her clothes, then laid across the bed.

Dynesha began playing with her breasts. She slid her hand down to her pussy. She was trying to get one off, but it wasn't seeming to work for her. Finally fed up, Dynesha got off the bed and put on her robe. She went into the kitchen to get a drink. As she stood there drinking a glass of water, she could see her next-door neighbor outside sitting on the hood of his car, smoking. She opened the door.

"What are you doing up this time of day? I thought you were a bat that only came out at night."

He put out the cigarette and walked over to the door. He kept staring at her firm breasts that were trying to break out of her robe.

"Nothing, I'm bored as fuck. I was supposed to chill with my boys, but they're still in class," he said, standing next to her.

"You want to come in?" Dynesha asked, looking at him and thinking in her mind that he would do.

Byron smiled and walked inside. He closed the door behind him. Dynesha walked over to the couch and sat down. He strolled over and sat down next to her. Neither one of them said anything. They just stared at each other for about thirty seconds. Taking the hint that she was giving him with her eyes, he stood up and removed his shirt, exposing his cut-up frame. His slick chest was nothing but muscle. He picked her up off the couch and pressed her against the wall. Dynesha wrapped her legs around his slender waist, and he kissed her crazily, carrying her to the bedroom.

He gently laid her down on the bed, then untied her robe, covering her neck and breast with his mouth. It felt so good to her, that her pussy began leaking.

"Yeesssss," she moaned, with her eyes closed.

He was so tender and sweet with each touch. Dynesha ran her hands over his huge back and up to his bald head. She could feel his belt buckle against her navel. Byron started grinding more rapidly. Dynesha playfully moved away from him, wanting the sensation to last.

He pulled her back into his grasp, straddling her and kissing down her legs. When he got to her slippers, he pulled them off and tossed them across the room. He held one of her feet in his hand, looked at her with a devilish smile, and began sucking each toe. Dynesha moaned at each suck. This was exactly what she needed right now.

"Come on. Fuck me, please," she moaned, grabbing his head and pulling him up on top of her body.

Byron pulled her robe all the way off and grabbed a fistful of her laced panties and snatched them from her body. He hopped out of his jeans with the speed of lightning, then his boxers.

"Slow down, I'm not going anywhere." Dynesha grinned at his naked body.

She grabbed and squeezed his ass as he slid inside her raw. He started pumping away, trying to go as deep as he possibly could. His breathing got heavier with each thrust. She let him know that he wasn't the only one enjoying it, by rotating her hips in circular motions, meeting him thrust for thrust. His groaning got louder, then he suddenly pulled out and buried his face between her thighs. Dynesha thought her body was about to erupt from the pleasure he was providing.

He moved back up and inserted his girth back inside her hot walls, slapping her hips until she couldn't take it anymore. Her whole body jerked into a maddening spasm. His release came next when his balls tightened up, shooting a little of his semen inside her before pulling out and squirting all over her stomach.

"Damn, that was better than I expected," Byron said, turning over and leaning back on the pillow.

"Don't get comfortable. It's time to go."

"How about we go another round?" He smiled, trying to play with her pussy.

Byron had been living next door to Dynesha for a while. He used to look out his window at her and her sisters come and go all the time. They looked better than any of the other girls on the block. Even their mom was still beautiful, and she was getting older and had a minor drug problem. They would never look in his direction when they saw him. That's why it fucked him up when she not only invited him into her crib, but also let him get some. He was hoping that this was the start of something good. That thought was quickly put to rest by her next words.

"No, you have to go now. This was only a one-time thing. I just needed to relieve some stress. Besides, your dick is a bit too little for me. Thanks for the quickie though."

Dynesha got off the bed and headed into the bathroom to take a shower. Byron put his clothes back on and left before she was done. Even though she tried to play him, he still left feeling good about himself.

~ ~ ~

"Man, where the fuck were you at when I called you?" Jake asked when Hot Dog walked in the room. He was lying in bed with an IV stuck in his arm. "That bitch tried to down me. It was a good thing her aim was off, or we probably wouldn't even be having this conversation."

"I was with shorty and didn't hear my phone, bro. I shouldn't have left you there by yourself with no heat on you. That was my bad, bro. I'm sorry," Hot Dog said. The look in his eyes showed that he was feeling bad that he chose pussy over watching his friend's back.

"Man, we good! I want to get out of here so

we can get this bitch though."

"What about the cops? Did they question you?"

"They tried, but I told them I didn't know shit. I said I came out to meet a girl at the bar, but she wasn't my type, so I left."

"Did those pigs buy your story?"

"I don't know, but I'm not trying to stick around to find out. I can tell you this, these muthafuckas stick together out here. Nobody said shit. They just told the cops that somebody wearing a mask tried to rob me, and when I started running, they began firing out of control."

"Damn, that bitch must be well known in the hood. Was her sister with her, or was she riding solo?"

"I wasn't paying attention once those shots started. I got the fuck out of there," Jake said, removing the IV from his arm. "Let's bounce before those detectives come back. We need to prioritize this shit and get out of this city. I want my shit."

"I'm with you, bro," Hot dog told him as they left the hospital.

Chapter Fourteen

The drug game had been treating me well once again. I was finally starting to feel myself. I was walking around the Steamtown Mall trying to find me something to wear, when out of the corner of my eye, I noticed someone staring at me. I looked up on the second floor, and Abby was standing there. What made me stare back was who she was standing there with. She was holding some little boy's hand. He was a spitting resemblance of her and looked like he was no more than five or six years old. That had me doing the math in my head, wondering if he was mine or not. I dismissed that notion once I saw who he really looked like.

I walked over to the escalator and went up to the second floor. They were still standing in the same area as if they were waiting for someone. I wanted my money, so I approached her and hoped she didn't make a scene.

"So who son is that?" I flat out asked.

"Jordan, you know who son this is. Look at him," Abby replied.

"I want a paternity test before I do anything for him, and where is my money?"

"Is that all you're worried about?" she said, getting so loud, that she was drawing attention toward us, just like I thought she would. "This is your fucking son. You should be worrying about him, not some damn money that I don't even have anymore because I used it to make sure he had everything he needed while you were away. You left me, Jordan, I didn't leave you."

Tears were starting to pour down her face. This was not the place I wanted to be having this conversation. I should have never said anything.

"Look, here's my number," I said, snatching her phone and storing it in. I then called my phone so I could get hers as well. "Call me tonight so we can set up a day to go get this maternity test done. I don't give a fuck about the money or who you're fucking. I do care if this is my son or not."

"Oh, so now you want to act like you care? Fuck you! Me and my baby will be just fine, with or without you."

"You know what—"

I was just about to snap out when some dude came out of the Boost Mobile store with some girl that looked like she was high. Come to think about it, so did Abby. Was she using drugs? Who was this dude they were with? I was going to confront them, but I needed to get to work soon, and one of my workers wanted me to pick up some money. I still had to go see about this new crib out in Green Ridge. I walked away, leaving Abby standing there with a puzzled look on her face.

~ ~ ~

After picking up the money off the worker, I headed over to the bank to deposit it. Once I left the bank, I drove around thinking about everything that had happened in the last few days. I tried to get Karma off my mind but couldn't shake the fact that she had fucked off on me. I knew she was guilty by how she had been acting toward me all of a sudden. Her whole demeanor had changed. She hadn't tried to call or text me since we had it out at her aunt and uncle's house.

I'm not going to lie; the thought of her laid up with someone else had me on tilt. Somehow I found myself in her neighborhood, cruising down her block, pulling up in front of her crib.

When I got to the door, I decided not to knock and used my key, so if she was in there fucking the next nigga, I could catch her in the act. When I opened the door, she was curled up on the couch under a blanket, watching the news.

Just looking at her had me ready to spazz out on her about what I found under her bed, but then I thought about my own secrets that I was keeping.

"Put my key on the table and get the fuck out of my house, Jordan!" She sat up and threw the blanket off.

"That nigga must be on his way over here, huh? Is that the reason you're trying to get rid of me?"

"What nigga?"

"The nigga that has been putting hickeys all over my girl's neck. You know what nigga I'm talking about!"

She made her way over to me and cocked her head to the side so I could see her neck.

"You're talking about that hickey? The one I got from my fucking flatiron hitting my neck? That's the hickey that got your ass switching up on me and talking to me like I'm some kind of ho. Boy miss me with that shit."

The same spot that had caught my attention at dinner the other day, was now a black burn mark. I almost felt like shit about wrongly accusing her, but then I thought about the text message she had sent saying she was busy.

"I see your little burn, but what was you doing Saturday night that had your ass too busy to answer my calls? Then you said you'd be by to see me tomorrow. What's up with that shit?"

"Oh my God, Jordan!" Karma snatched her phone off the table, dialed a number, put her phone on speaker, and then waited for the person to answer. "Hey, Ry Ry. Sorry to bug you—"

"Who the fuck is Ry Ry?" I yelled, interrupting her conversation.

Karma cut her eyes at me, then continued, "Like I was saying, I'm sorry to bug you, but can you please tell Jordan what we did Saturday night, until the wee hours of the morning?"

"Well if he really wants to know, he should have came over here too. We could have used his help cleaning up all this bullshit Mommy had in the garage. It was all our toys and clothes that she got us when we were little. I didn't realize how much stuff we had as kids. We were some lucky and spoiled muthafuckas, Karm. We had to pack all that stuff up and send it to the Salvation Army. We had our hands full."

Ry Ry, who I realized was her sister Rynesha, kept going on about what they found in the garage and how they use to wear each other's clothes, until Karma finally cut her off.

"Thank you, Sis. I'll be over to go over those papers with you probably tomorrow."

"Karma," Rynesha said before she hung up, "make sure this is the last time you call me to prove where you were for some fucking nigga. If you don't have trust, you don't have nothing and shouldn't be together at all. I think you should really think about your relationship with him, because when someone points the finger at you, there's always three more pointing back at them. The person that accuses the next of doing wrong is usually the one doing all the wrong in the first place. They're reacting off their own guilt. We still never even met him yet. What kind of shit is that?"

Without her being straightforward and saying it, Rynesha had just told Karma that I was the one out there doing dirt, and I could tell that she was soaking it all up too.

"You know my whereabouts; now tell me about yours since you want to judge me," Karma demanded after she ended the call.

I wasn't expecting this shit to flip on me like this. I had been sure that she was fucking someone else, and now I had all the proof that she wasn't. How stupid was I looking right now? That still didn't explain why she didn't answer my calls.

"Why didn't you answer your phone or at least call me back after you were done?"

"Jordan, you must be tripping off of something. You talk reckless to me, then expect me to just forget it like nothing happened? Come on with that. Where were you? When I left from my sister's house, I came to your room. I had the office make me a key card. I fell asleep and woke up at six in the morning to come home and get ready to meet a client that had to give me the retainer fee for her husband. So I know you stayed out all night. Who the fuck were you with?"

I didn't know what to say or do. My eyes searched the room for answers, but all I thought about was how I was the one out there being deceiving. Karma had chocolate candy, and strawberry ice cream on the table with a tablespoon stuck in it. I was about to lie, but decided not to.

"One of my coworkers at the club invited me to his birthday party. I didn't have a clue that we were going to be in Philly, until we were on the turnpike. The party was over around four, and then we went to get something to eat at the Penrose Diner while he sobered up enough to drive us back. I made it back to my room at ten minutes to seven and went to sleep until your uncle called."

"Is that right? Well you shouldn't have a problem calling this person and verifying it like I did," Karma said, placing her hands on her hips.

I couldn't call Cash, because the real reason we went out there wasn't just for the party, but also to meet up with somebody about some more business. I tried to think of a way out of this, then thought of something that might work. I pulled my phone out and pulled up the internet so I could look up the number to the club, and dialed it. I put the phone on speaker, just like she had done.

"Thank you for calling Vanity Grand. This Mark, how may I help you?"

I didn't know that the owner's name was Mark, but I knew it was him by his squeaky, girlish voice.

"What's up, Mark? This is Jay, the guy who came to the party with Trevor." I didn't say Cash's name because he liked to be incognito.

"Oh yes. How are you my friend?"

"I'm good. I was just telling a friend of mine how your club is the best one Philly has to offer, so she could book an event with you. I was trying to figure out what time y'all closed, because I couldn't remember if we stayed to closing or if we left before."

"Oh no, Jay. You guys left at closing. We shut things down around three, but we don't close until four."

"That's what I needed to know. Thank you!"

I hung up before he could say anything that would get me into any more trouble. Before I got the chance to get in Karma's ass for wrongly accusing me, she was already wrapping her arms around my neck and kissing my lips. The warmth of her body was mesmerizing me.

"I'm sorry, baby. You were just acting weird. The phone and car thing without telling me you were getting either threw me off. Promise me you'll keep me in the loop from this point on."

"I'm sorry too, babe, and I promise to always let you know shit beforehand," I lied. How could I tell her about the baby? I was going to wait until I knew for sure first; then we could cross that bridge at that time.

I picked her up and carried her to the bed, thanking God with every step for getting me out of this one. Just when I got ready to lay her down and reward her for keeping what belonged to me as mine, my phone started ringing. Not my personal line, but my business one. Since all the calls were forwarded to my personal phone whenever I wasn't in the car, I set a special ringtone for it. I didn't answer it, knowing if I did, we'd be right back to arguing. I decided to please her with my tongue real quick, then make a break for it.

"Yeesssss, baaabbby," she moaned when I spread her legs, placing them on my shoulder.

I dug into her kitty like I was eating a full-course meal. The slurping sounds must have excited her, because before I knew it, she was leaking all over my face. She tried to pull away, but I held on to her, paying special attention to her clit. My tongue was a miracle worker, and

Karma was the recipient.

"Can you keep it wet for me until I get back?" I asked after feeling her thighs tighten around my face for the third time.

"What? Where are you going now?" Karma unwrapped her legs from around my head and scooted her bottom away from my face.

"Look at the time, baby. I have to be to work at seven. The only reason I came here first was because I needed to see you. You were invading my thoughts, and I didn't want to go to work like that."

Damn, the lies just kept shooting out of my mouth. The crazy part about it, it was a really good lie. She didn't know I had called off for the night so I could get money.

Karma looked at her clock and realized that I was telling the truth. She went into the bathroom and returned with a soapy washcloth.

"Well, clean up before you leave."

"Naw, I'm going to leave your scent on my face for motivation," I replied, hitting her with a bedroom smile.

I leaned in to kiss her goodbye, and she pushed my face away with her hands. "I don't eat pussy, you do!"

"But you like it, don't you?"

"Fuck you!" She smiled, throwing a pillow at me as I headed out the door.

I called Cash when I made it out to my car, to see what was up. He didn't answer, but I noticed he had left a message to meet him at the apartment in Green Ridge. I threw my car in drive and headed straight over to the spot. He knew the realtor that was going to rent the apartment to me, so I kind of got a discount.

Once I squared everything up with the realtor and she gave me the keys, me and Cash headed over to the stash house to grab some work.

"Grab that brick out of the refrigerator. This is your show now, Jay," Cash said, wrapping his arm around my neck. "This will prove if you're ready to take over the business or not."

Usually we did all the drops together, but I would collect money by myself. I was wondering why he wanted me to drop the packages off now, but I didn't question him. I did as I was told. That drop was all it took to prove to Cash that I could handle this shit by myself. I made sure niggas were running a tight ship under my command, and we expanded all over PA and

Delaware. We were untouchable. My PO left me alone and only called once a month to check on me. I felt like I was back where I left off at, but sometimes, all good things come to an end.

Chapter Fifteen

Over the next two months, a lot changed for me. I saved up over $350,000 dollars, bought a new car, and moved into a house. I also learned the difference between Cash and Trevor. Cash was more subtle about getting his money, and Trevor was all out with it. Whatever it took to watch the paper pile up, Trevor was all for it. He even started fucking with some niggas out in Jersey, and I wanted in. He said they'd buy up everything he came with, and they always wanted more. I told him that I had a few keys and could get more from our plug if we needed it. A couple hours later we were in Jersey, ready to make a big deal with some major players.

"We're meeting up with those niggas tomorrow at this strip club downtown. My connect said we didn't give him enough notice on getting two kilos of heroin, but he'd have the money for us by then."

I didn't care if he needed an extra day to get his money up as long as we went home empty-handed. We checked in to a hotel since we would be there until at least tomorrow night, then headed to Cherry Hill Mall to find something to wear. We had separate rooms just in case one of us got lucky. In my case, I wasn't too worried about getting lucky unless it was with my boo at home. The only way we would be doing that right now was by video chat.

At first she didn't like the idea of me coming out here, but I told her it was to promote the club and that my boss was paying me double-time for volunteering. I told her that I had something special for us when I returned, and she got excited.

The next evening, me and Trevor were dressed and ready to hit the club. Trevor had talked to the connect and told him that we were on our way. The club was packed with more men than women, but it was still early, and more women were arriving. Niggas were sitting at tables and booths cliqued up.

"This shit is packed."

90)

"Damn right, and there's some bad bitches up in here too," Trevor said, looking around at all the half-naked women trying to dance for the customers.

You could tell who didn't fuck with whom by the way they were ice grilling each other. I wasn't here to check out niggas though. The hos in here were too bad not to pay any attention to. Karma would be pissed if she saw me now. These strippers were cornbread fed, and judging by how thick and solid they were, you could tell they loved steaks and potatoes. Asses roamed free, like the club was a farm full of horses and donkeys. I got a peek of a bow-legged black stallion with her eyes on me and urged her with my finger to come my way.

"Let me get a private dance," I said.

She licked her full, cherry-colored lips, swung all twenty inches or better of her sewed-in hair over her right shoulder, and said, "It took you long enough! I got the perfect spot."

She took me upstairs and pulled back a red curtain. Sitting back on the couch was Trevor and two other niggas, making the drop. I came in just in time to watch the money and product switch hands.

"This is my nigga, Jay, right here. He's the nigga next to the nigga. Whatever y'all need, he will make sure to supply," Trevor said, introducing me to the others.

"What's good with you, Jay? I'm Bruce, and this is my right-hand man, Rav. Tell me you brought more than just this with you."

I shook both of their hands while shaking my head no and sat down. Trevor didn't say anything as they all waited for me to elaborate.

"I can bring some more this way in a day or two. I just need to know what you're trying to get. It ain't shit to drive it back here to you."

"We'll get at Trevor when we're ready," Bruce said, giving Rav a weird look.

I hadn't noticed it, but the bitch who had brought me upstairs had left and was now making her way back into the room.

"Is y'all done yet, Bruce? Y'all fucking up my privacy."

The bowlegged girl, named Diamond, grabbed my hand so I wouldn't leave when everyone else did. When the room was clear, she went straight to work. She was on my lap, naked, popping her shit slowly, moving her body like a snake, and showing me just how flexible she was as she wrapped her ankles around the back of her head, exposing her thick-lipped pussy. I was enjoying the show, but something about the scene had a déjà vu feeling to it.

"This ain't the only kinda private I give, daddy." She grabbed my hand and rammed it in her pussy. "If you want to know what I really feel like, this is just a sample."

"Damn," was all I could say, while she squeezed her pussy muscles as tight as she could around my three fingers and made it pulsate to the beat of the music.

"Just tell me when you're staying the night, and Diamond will be there fulfilling any fantasy you wish."

"Like this?" I asked.

"You better know it!"

I removed my fingers from her pussy and wiped them across her nipples. Like a cat at a bowl of milk, she licked her juices away, then cleaned my fingers off with her mouth. My pants woke up, ready to tear into her ass, but I wouldn't fuck up on Karma twice. My second head didn't want me to, so I pushed the freaky bitch off my lap.

"I'm good." I dug in my pockets and made a thousand dollars rain on her ass as she sat on the carpeted floor, looking up at me like I had lost my mind.

I went downstairs, and Trevor was sitting

with Bruce and Rav in front of the main stage. He motioned for me to step away with him.

"I put the money in the dashboard. Why don't you take it back to the room, so we won't be here with all these bands on us? I'll take an Uber back to the room in an hour. I'm just finishing up some other business with these niggas."

I wasn't with that idea at first, because I didn't want to leave him there by himself. I also knew he was right about having all this money here at the club with all these thirsty niggas.

"Okay, I'm out!"

I took the keys from him and headed out of the club. About an hour and a half later, Trevor came through the door with Diamond tucked under his arm.

"You straight?" I asked. He looked her body up and down with lust in his eyes and nodded his head yes.

"I'm about to be," he said while kissing her on the neck.

I cut the TV off and rolled me a dutch. Halfway through smoking it, I heard the sounds of the headboard slamming against the wall and Diamond screaming like Trevor was beating the breaks off her, and this caused me to turn the

TV back on and raise the volume to high.

"Hit that shit, Trev," I said to myself, laughing.

The sound of Diamond's moans sent my pants bulging up. I wished Karma were here with me. I started rubbing my man the way she would to let me know she wanted some. My hand didn't feel as good as hers, but my imagination was a muthafucka. I freed my dick from its captor and spit on my hands to replicate the feeling of her mouth. As I stroked it, I replayed the nasty shit Karma said whenever she made me her lollipop, and then came the knocks on the door, right before I could give her a taste of my cream filling.

I thought it might be room service, so I went to the peephole with my dick swinging, intent on finishing the job after I sent them off, but it was Bruce and Rav. I tucked my shit away and wiped my hand on my shirt before opening the door.

"What's up? Trevor is in the other room handling some business. Y'all can have a seat on the couch while I go get him." I turned my back and took a step toward Trevor's room.

The sound of one being put in the chamber sent me whirling around to find Rav holding his gun in my face and Bruce nudging me with an assault rifle.

"Naw, you have a seat, nigga. We'll go get Trevor."

It took everything in me not to piss on myself. I couldn't believe what was transpiring right before my eyes right now, and I couldn't do a damn thing.

"What the fuck is going on?" I asked.

"Don't make this harder than it needs to be. Just do what we say and you may make it out of here alive."

Rav forced me to the couch and kept me there at gunpoint, while Bruce went to retrieve Trevor. A few seconds later, Trevor came crawling into the room, naked, with Diamond kicking him in the ass, her gun pointed at him. I could hear Bruce rummaging through shit in Trevor's room.

"Y'all just sit here quiet and don't try no nut shit, and I promise y'all will be able to go back to Scranton in one piece." Rav was talking to both of us, but he kept his eyes on Trevor.

"Nigga, I thought y'all niggas could be trusted. I heard y'all Jersey muthafuckas weren't nothing but some bitches—"

Diamond hit Trevor in his mouth before he could get the rest of his words out. Blood began to seep from his mouth, along with a tooth.

"Nigga, I'm not from Jersey, and I'm sure as hell ain't no bitch, so watch your fucking mouth."

The little bitch had some hands on her, because within seconds, Trevor's lip swelled up like he had an allergic reaction to something. Rav pointed his gun at his head, and Diamond switched places with him and pointed hers at me. I knew we weren't going to make it out of here alive because they let us see their faces. I let my street smarts kick in, as I searched around the room for anything I could use to defend myself, but couldn't find anything. Our handguns were in the drawer, and the big shit was in the trunk.

About two minutes later, Bruce came out of the room and gave Rav an inventory of what he had found. It wasn't much though.

"Thirteen hundred dollars and some weed, that's all this nigga had!"

"Nigga, search again. They have to have the money in here somewhere. Matter of fact, I'll go look."

Bruce came up and pointed his rifle at

Trevor. Rav put his hands on the top of the rifle and pushed it down, inches away from Trevor's exposed dick.

"Bruce, if this nigga says anything, send him back to Scranton neutered. He's been trying to act tough, but we know it's just a front."

I had learned from seeing how easily Diamond hit Trevor not to say shit. I kept my eyes on her ass because this bitch was the true definition of why bitches couldn't be trusted. I guess my stares were making her uncomfortable, because she put the gun closer to my head.

"I should shoot your ass for shoving your nasty-ass fingers up my pussy like I'm some kind of ho."

Bruce reached over and popped me in the head with the handle of his rifle. I fell over, feeling dazed, and a knot started to grow where the weapon had met my head.

"Fuck, boy, you touched my bitch? You better hope I don't smoke your nut ass."

Diamond smiled as if the fact that Bruce had called her his bitch was an honor, instead of taking it as a form of disrespect. What he didn't know was Diamond really was thinking that

Bruce was out of his mind if he thought she belonged to him.

"I didn't touch her, she grabbed my—"

Diamond's fist shut my mouth as Rav came out of Trevor's room empty-handed. He went over to my closet, and three minutes later, he was holding my backpack up in the air.

"Bingo! This nigga had our money, plus another fifty grand in here. Tie their asses up," Rav said. "I'm going to get the car. Take care of this shit, and hurry up."

I knew what that meant, thinking about what we did to those niggas that came for us at the hotel. We were as good as dead. They made Trevor lie on his stomach, a few feet from me. I turned my head the other way, and that's when I saw it. Trevor was always prepared for anything. He had stuck a gun under the bed. It was close enough for me to grab it, but would I have enough time to get a shot off or not? They were so focused on tying Trevor up because I played like I was hurt, that they didn't see me sliding my hand up under the bed and grabbing the gun.

BOOM! BOOM! BOOM!

The sound was so deafening that even

Trevor jumped. Bruce's body hit the floor hard. Diamond tried to turn toward me, but before she could aim her weapon, I was sending four rounds her way. Two to the chest, one to the neck, and a kill shot to the forehead. I weakly stood up and put two more rounds into Bruce's body, making sure he was gone. By this time, Trevor was already on his feet packing everything up and grabbing the other guns from the drawer.

"Take anything that will implicate us, and let's go," he said, throwing a shirt and sweatpants on. "We have to get downstairs and catch that other muthafucka."

I didn't say a word the whole time we were on the elevator. All I wanted to do right now was get our money back. Soon as we stepped off the elevator, I noticed a car parked near the side entrance.

"Is that his car right there?" I asked, pulling Trevor back so he didn't see us.

"Yeah, that's that muthafucka. You go out the front and come around while I go this way and catch him off guard. Be careful and don't let anyone see you."

I nodded my head and eased out the hotel.

Rav sat in his Yukon, smoking some of the weed he took from us, oblivious to his surroundings. He glanced up just as I was approaching from the front. Before he could reach for his weapon, Trevor had his gun aimed at his head.

"Move and you die," he said in a low voice. Rav put his hands up in the air.

By this time I was already on the passenger side, grabbing what belonged to us, and the work that we sold them earlier. Once I was safely out of the car, Trevor shot Rav once in the head. His body leaned over into the passenger seat. We hopped in our car, and Trevor peeled off, heading back to Scranton. We didn't even realize that the eye in the sky had been recording the whole scene that took place outside. If we knew what this trip was about to cost us, we never would have taken that ride.

Chapter Sixteen

***

I was on my way home from work when I pulled into the gas station to get gas. As I was getting out the car, I spotted an old friend looking through something in his trunk.

"Does your parole officer know what you got in that bag?" I said, walking up on Reek.

Me and Reek hadn't seen each other since we were cellies at Camp Hill. I was wondering how the hell he got out of a life bid. He must have gotten his sentence overturned or something. That's something that I would have to ask him later. Right now, I was just glad to see him. He looked over his shoulder at me while he was closing the bag.

"Who the fuck is that?" he said, reaching for what I knew was a gun. I quickly announced myself, before he made a mistake and pulled the trigger.

"Damn, Reek, you don't recognize your brother when you see him, nigga?"

He tucked his gun back in his waist, closed his trunk, and ran over to me for an open-arm hug. He had me in a bear hug, squeezing me so tight that I almost suffocated.

"Damn, Jay. Look at you, bro! You getting old on me. Looks like you've been eating good out here," Reek said, looking at my Infinity truck.

"I can say the same for you, pushing that Benz."

"Damn, it's so much I have to tell you, lil bro. I thought that I would be in that cage for the rest of my life, but look where I'm at now, all because I fought this fucking system and won, as you can see," he said, pointing to his ride. "Man, I never gave up on myself, and with the help of some very important people, I have a second chance on life. And to answer your question, I don't have to report to anybody but myself."

"That's what's up! I have to be on paper for a few more years; then hopefully I will be done with this fucked-up system." We talked for a few more minutes, until I received a strange text message from my girl.

"Come home now please! 911."

I knew something was wrong because she never had texted me with that kind of message before. I quickly tried to call her back, but it went straight to voicemail. I tried again, with the same result.

"Bro, I have to get home. I will hit your jack later and we can hit the club and kick it," I said, giving him my number.

"You straight?" he asked, seeing the concerned look on my face.

"Yeah I'm straight," I told him, because I wasn't sure what was going on yet. I hopped in my car and headed over to my girl's crib.

~ ~ ~

I arrived at Karma's in record time. I grabbed my burner out of the glove compartment and headed inside with caution, thinking that somebody was holding her hostage to get to me. When I walked in, she was sitting on the couch crying her heart out. As soon as she saw me, she jumped up and ran into my arms. I held her tightly wondering what was going on. Her tears were flowing uncontrollably.

"Karma, what is it, baby?"

Her sobbing slowed down just enough for her to look up at me. "Somebody killed my sister." She started crying again.

I didn't know what to say or do at that moment. I never got the chance to meet her sisters in person yet, so it was mindboggling to hear that one of them had been murdered.

"When? Where? How? What happened?" Questions were flying out of my mouth at a rapid speed, but Karma was in so much pain that she couldn't answer any of them. All I could do was hold her until she was ready to talk.

About an half hour later, she was finally ready to tell me what happened. She said her sister and some dude were found dead in a hotel room. They had been robbed and shot multiple times. I felt so bad for her and couldn't imagine the pain she was going through. She asked me to take her to her mother's house to be with her mom and sister.

"Of course I will. I'm so sorry, baby, for your loss."

I helped her into the car, and we headed to her mom's house. I hated seeing my girl in so much pain, knowing that I couldn't do anything to take it away right now. If I knew who was behind this, I would kill them myself, just to make her pain go away. Even though I never got the chance to meet her, I knew that they were really close with each other.

When we got there, I found a parking spot and then got out to open the door for her. She held my arm tightly as we made our way up the steps. She pulled out her set of keys and unlocked the door. As soon as we walked into the living room, her mom rushed to her.

"Oh, baby," her mom sobbed.

"Mommy," Karma began crying all over again.

I stood back by the door, allowing them all the time they needed to mourn together. I couldn't believe how much her and her mother looked alike. Karma was just a younger version. Seeing her, I could tell that her sisters were probably just as beautiful. I walked over and sat down on the couch.

"Hi, I'm Karma's mother," she said, seeing me sitting there. I stood up and gave her a hug. "He's a cutie baby."

"I'm truly sorry for your loss."

"Thank you! Would you like something to drink?"

"Sure!" She brought me a can of Pepsi. "Thank you!"

We were all sitting there talking about what happened, when I heard someone else walk in the door. My back was to them, so I didn't see who it was until she rushed over and hugged her mother and sister. It was Karma's older sister. I only could see her from behind, until she let go of their embrace. I damn near choked on the soda when she looked in my direction.

"It can't be!" I thought to myself looking at this girl standing a few feet from me. I remembered Karma telling me she had twin sisters.

"Baby, this is my big sister Rynesha. Ry, this is my man, Jordan."

"It's a pleasure to finally meet the man my baby sister is head over heels for. Too bad it's under these current circumstances."

I didn't know what to do at that moment. The girl I killed out in Jersey was my future wife's sister. This was another secret I would have to keep from her. Just when I thought things couldn't get any worse, my parole officer called me and left a voice message to come see her ASAP for a urine test. If I took a piss test now, it would surely come back hot. Why was she suddenly asking for one out of the blue, anyway? I figured if I could hold off for two more days, I'd have the weekend to clean up. For the rest of the time that I was there, I felt like shit, but these skeletons would go to the grave with me if I could help it.

"We have to go to Jersey to claim Dynesha's body," Karma's mom said.

Karma asked if I could go with them, but I made up an excuse using my PO's message as confirmation, and she bought it. I knew if I went back to Jersey, I would risk being arrested, and that just was not going to happen.

"Call me when you're on your way back home, okay?" I said, giving her a kiss and hug before walking out the door. Her tears were melting me because of the guilt trip I was feeling.

When I left her mother's house, I called Trevor and told him that we had to meet up and talk ASAP. He needed to know what I just found out, and figure out our next move.

"Damn, what the fuck!" I yelled, hitting my steering wheel.

Chapter Seventeen

I felt like I was trapped in love. At one end, I wanted to tell Karma that her sister died at the hands of my gun because I was back in the game. Then on the other end, telling her would not only break her heart, but also end our relationship. I was in a fucked-up predicament.

I was so caught up in my own thoughts that I didn't hear my phone ringing. When I pulled up to Cash's crib, I hit the horn twice and he came out. He had on his workout gear, which meant he was just in the basement working out. He opened the passenger side and got in.

"What's up, Jay? Trevor told me about the incident out Jersey, and he told me who was involved. Are you sure that her other sisters had nothing to do with that?"

That thought never once crossed my mind until Cash asked me. Then, just as easily, it was gone. There was no way Karma had anything to do with what her sister was into. She would never do that, or would she? That's when that fucking briefcase that was under her bed popped back into my head.

"No, she works very hard. She had nothing to do with it."

"You sure? 'Cause you know these bitches ain't shit, nigga," he replied. "I know that's your girl and all, but you have to keep an open—"

"She don't know nothing," I snapped back. Cash had never seen me this mad before, but he definitely got the message once he saw my face.

"Take me out Dickson City real quick so I can pick some food up for my snake," Cash said, dropping the subject.

As we drove down 81, my phone went off letting me know that I had another message. It was from Juan, one of our workers who we left in charge of the stash house in Valleyview. Cash had just given him work, so there wasn't a reason for him to be calling. I called him back, but the phone went straight to voicemail. I checked the message he had left, which was about two minutes long.

The only thing that could be heard was rambling, like his phone had called me by accident while it was in his pocket. I listened to the message in its entirety; then I heard the reason for his call. Right before the call ended, I heard gunshots ring out.

"What the fuck!" I said out loud. "Listen to this!" I put the phone on speaker and played the message back for Cash to hear, at the same time turning around and heading to the projects.

"I don't hear shit, Jay."

"Shhhh, keep listening!"

When the gunshots went off, Cash looked at me, then said, "Floor this shit."

I didn't care about getting pulled over by any cops at that moment. We needed to get there fast to figure out what had happened. When we pulled up to the house, Juan's car was still parked in the lot. I did a visual inspection, and everything looked intact. We couldn't see any bullet holes outside the door, nor were the police outside, taping the area off like it was a crime scene. The lights were on inside as usual, and I could hear Juan's music blasting. That's how he worked when he was there. He played music, watching the girls bag up.

I knocked on the door. Cash pointed out the door frame to me. It had been kicked in, and the wood was cracked where the door lock would have been secured in it. Cash used his shirt to turn the doorknob, and the door opened. As soon as we walked in, we knew something wasn't right because the house was empty. It was one of our rules that someone always had to be at the crib while product was there, even if the workers weren't bagging up.

I went to check the bedroom, because that was where we had the dope stashed after it was bagged up. I turned the knob using my shirt as Cash had done when we came in, and saw that all the floorboards had been pulled up. The ice packs were still there, but not one package of heroin could be found. The room wasn't fucked up like somebody was searching for the shit. They knew exactly where to look.

"Jay, come here!"

Cash was standing with one foot in the hall and his other in the bathroom. He kept turning his head from the bathroom to the hallway as I made my way over to him. I could hear the shower running and noticed steam coming into the hallway. The curtain at the front of the shower was closed to prevent the water from hitting the floor, but toward the back, I could see one fully dressed and one half-naked body stacked on top of each other, in a tub full of blood. I pushed the curtain open with my arm, and there was Juan. On top of him was one of the girls that worked for us. They were both dead.

From what I could tell, Juan had been shot through his head and chest by something big. He had burn marks around his right eye, and the left eyeball was missing. I couldn't tell how the girl died, but I could see that three of her fingers were burnt off to the knuckle. I grabbed a towel off the rack, lifted the toilet lid, and threw up everything I had consumed that day. I ran into the hallway to get myself together and get some fresh air.

"All the work is gone!" I said to Cash as he made his way back into the hallway.

"They tortured them in the kitchen until they talked. There's blood all over the stove, and there's an eyeball stuck on a screwdriver that is sitting on the kitchen countertop."

Cash's stomach was stronger than mine. I had seen some gruesome shit before, but I guess you can say that this just caught me off guard. He didn't even throw up, but he kept jerking his head like he would. He went and looked at the lifted floorboards in the bedroom, then made his way back into the bathroom. He took the cellphones from both bodies and stuck them in his pocket.

"We have to take anything they may have on them that can link shit back to us. Make sure there's no drugs on them, so when the police notify their families, they don't see the real reason this happened. Put the boards back down like they was, and let's bounce."

We moved quickly, and when we walked out, we had hoodies over our heads. We made sure nobody saw what we looked like and that nobody was outside watching us drive away. As a precaution, Cash told me that I had to get rid of my car. It was my trap vehicle, so it didn't matter. Just because we didn't see anybody watching, didn't mean they weren't.

When we were far enough away from the stash house, we stopped a fiend that was passing by. Cash used her phone and called the police, telling them to go check out the address, then hung up. I don't know if he was paranoid or if it was part of him being cautious, but he made sure to wipe his prints off and paid her fifty dollars before jumping back in the car.

"That shit was an inside job, bro, I'm telling

you," I said to Cash. I had seen something like that before and may have known who it was even. "I have to see who else was supposed to be there with Juan."

Cash named a few people that usually were there. None seemed like that type, but in this game you couldn't trust anyone. Then he said a name that I recognized. It was one of my old friend's cousins.

"When did she work at the house? I don't remember seeing her there."

"She just started a few days ago. Why? You think she had something to do with it?" Cash asked me, seeing that I was in deep thought about something.

"I don't know, but I'm going to keep an eye on her."

"You do that. Drop me off at my car; I have shit to do."

I could tell things were going to get worse before they got better. Whether we would be able to weather the storm or not, remained to be seen.

~ ~ ~

The days that followed all seemed gray and lifeless. I couldn't think straight and was fucking up left and right, but my biggest fuck-up wasn't discovered until the night I stayed at Karma's house by myself, because she had to stay late at work.

Karma texted me, "Sorry I'm working late. My boss needs us to finish these briefs for an upcoming trial next week. I'll be home before midnight. ♡ u."

"♥ u too!" I texted back.

I was sitting on the couch with my phone, on the internet, looking at all the Instagram pictures that people were posting, with one hand in my pants when I heard a knock on the door. When I looked out the window, Rynesha was standing there. I hadn't seen her since they buried her twin sister three weeks ago.

"Hey, Jay, is my sister home yet?" she asked when I opened the door to let her in.

"Not yet! She said she'll be home before midnight. You can wait for her if you want. I ordered pizza that should be here soon."

"Okay, but if she don't come home soon, I'm out."

Once the pizza came, we ate, drank, and talked while watching *Love Island.* I fell asleep on the couch. The liquor must have had me feeling good because I thought I felt someone massaging my dick. When I opened my eyes, Rynesha had her hand inside my pants, jerking me off. I tried to move away, but my body wouldn't respond. When she saw that I wasn't disagreeing, she pulled my dick out of my shorts, then got in between my legs, wrapping her lips around it. Rynesha's mouth was wet and warm. My balls tensed up as she worked me over.

"What are you doing?" I managed to get out between moans, but she didn't answer.

Instead, she stood up in front of me and pulled off her tights. She had one of the prettiest pussies I'd ever seen. Only Karma's looked better. Rynesha stood over top of me on the couch, with her love box inches away from my face, inviting me to suck on her clit that was pulsating between her swollen lips. Later I could blame it on the alcohol, but right now I was so horny that I grabbed her waist and pulled her body down on my face. Her pussy smelled like strawberries, and I ate it up. Her body started convulsing as she had one of many to come orgasms.

"Oh God, eat that shit," she purred softly.

I stopped and pulled her down on my dick. Her pussy was so warm that I thought I would bust after the first two pumps. Just when I was starting to get a rhythm, she stopped me and pulled out.

"Hold up! You need to put a condom on."

"I don't have any," I told her, trying to stick it back in. "Come on! I know how to pull out."

She wasn't feeling it at first, but I was persistent. Rynesha finally gave in, and guided my dick back into her super-soaked hole. We fucked so hard that I sweated all the liquor out of my system. That's when reality kicked in. I felt so guilty about what I was doing, that I stopped in mid-stroke and pushed her up off of me. I stood up and fixed my shorts.

"Really? You just gonna stop like that?" she said disappointedly.

"This is not right. My girl is your sister."

"That wasn't stopping you a few minutes ago," she said, reaching for me, but I moved away.

"Chill. You need to get dressed. Karma will be here soon," I said, checking my phone to see if she texted me yet.

Rynesha gave up and picked her tights up off the floor. Once she was dressed, she walked toward the door and then turned back toward me.

"The dick wasn't even as good as she said it was. Get your weight up, player." She smiled then walked out the door.

Chapter Eighteen

I left the club around seven and was heading home to spend the day with my boo. Me and Karma hadn't spent that much time together because she worked during the day and I worked at night. I decided to take this weekend off so we could maybe take a trip out to Philly and see my family. Besides that, I was still feeling guilty about a lot of things. It seemed like I was living a double life that she didn't know about. I was going to do everything in my power to make sure she never found out about my demons. She sent me a picture of her wearing a new thong set and told me to hurry home and help her take it off. I texted her back with a smiley face and told her I was on my way.

As I drove home, I noticed that I missed a call from Ant. I called him back, expecting to hear that he was done with the stash houses. Instead, he hit me with some bullshit that wiped the smile off my face.

"I was on my way home when I realized that I left my bag at the spot. When I pulled back up,

I noticed four niggas robbing the joint. I ducked behind the house till they were done. Now I'm following them niggas to see where they're going."

"Is Preme okay?" I asked.

"Yeah. He gave up the product, and those niggas tied him up. Go get Preme and then call me to see where I am, Jay."

I hit the gas heading to the spot that was robbed. On my way, I called Cash and told him what was going on and to be ready to act when I called back with a destination. When I got there, I found Preme tied up, with newspaper stuffed in his mouth. I removed the newspaper and untied him.

"Jay, a nigga ain't never been this happy to see you. How did you know we got hit?"

"Ant left his bag, and when he pulled up, he saw them niggas tying y'all up. He following them now. Then I'm meeting him to see where they went."

"I'm going too. Them niggas are good as dead!"

He rubbed his wrists for a second, then grabbed a chair out of the kitchen and climbed into the attic. He came back down with more guns and bullets than Rambo.

"Ant said you weren't by yourself when they robbed you. Who else was here?"

"It was me, Brad, and the lil bitch that worked at the other spot. They took the bitch with them and made Brad show them where the other spots were. Brad ain't no bitch, so he's probably dead by now."

When he said it was the same bitch that was at the other spot, I instantly knew who he was talking about. It wasn't just a coincidence anymore. She was working with her cousin, and whoever else, I'm not sure. If they were really behind this, I wouldn't hesitate to put a bullet in them myself.

Preme was mad, but I knew he was right. Robbing and killing went hand in hand when dealing with this drug shit, and it was part of the game. We hopped in the car and headed over to meet up with Ant. He was standing at the corner when we pulled up. He hopped in the back seat of my car.

"Whoever was driving dropped two of the niggas and the bitch off at that crib right there," Ant said, pointing to the house on Wayne Avenue.

This was definitely the block where my old friend lived. I wondered why he would want to rob me though. I left them out here eating and they shitted on me, not the other way around. I came home with nothing and busted my ass to get back, and this is what it came down to? Fuck them, they were gonna pay for this shit.

"Y'all ready to go get our shit?" I said, cocking my gun.

"Fuck yeah, I'm ready!"

"Me too!" Preme said.

We all walked toward the house as casually as possible, until we reached the porch. I told Ant and Preme to go around back, while I went up to the front door. I tapped lightly on the door and waited for someone to answer. A couple of seconds later, I heard the lock being turned, and then the door opened.

"Damn, long time no see," Stizz said.

"Yeah, you too! You mind if I come in?"

I could tell that he was nervous, but he stood to the side so I could enter. His cousin and another dude was sitting on the couch all boo'd up when I stepped into the living room. She looked like she had seen a ghost when I spoke.

"What's going on, Mia?" I said, sitting down

in the chair across from where they were sitting. "I was worried about you when they told me the stash house got hit and the niggas took you and Brad. I see you made it out okay though."

"Yeah! They threw me out of the car after they drove around for a while," she said nervously. I could tell by her whole demeanor that she was lying through her teeth, but I let her continue to dig herself deeper in the hole. "I called my cousin, and him and Chris came to pick me up."

"What happened to Brad?"

"I don't know. They took him with them."

Out of the corner of my eye, I could see that Ant and Preme had snuck in the back door and were waiting on my signal. Chris had one of his arms around Mia's neck, and the other was inside one of the cushions on the couch. That meant he was toting a weapon, so once shit hit the fan, he would have to be the first to go.

"See, Mia, this is what I find hard to believe. You have only been working for us a short time, and in that time, all kinds of shit has been happening. Then your trifling ass is related to this nigga who I've known most of my life. The same nigga who basically left me for dead when

I was locked up."

"Yo, don't talk to my bitch like that," Chris said aggressively. I quickly shut that shit down. Before he could get his gun out, I gave Ant the signal.

POP!

Chris's head went forward, knocking his body to the floor. Mia screamed, holding her face, and before Stizz could reach his gun, Preme had already had the drop on him.

"Go ahead, nigga, make a fucking move and you'll be joining that pussy in the afterlife." Stizz put his hands in the air with fear in his eyes.

"So I'm only going to ask you this one time; then I'm going to torture you just like you did my workers, but I can promise you that it will hurt a lot more," I said, leaning forward in the chair so I was directly in Mia's face. "Where is my shit?"

"Jordan, I swear I don't know what you are talking about. Please, I didn't do—"

"Wrong answer."

BOOM!

"Ahhhhh," Mia's scream was deafening as she held her kneecap. I put my gun to her other knee, pressing down on it with my finger on the trigger. "It's upstairs in the back room in the closet."

I gave Preme a nod and he ran upstairs to search for our shit. He was back within in minutes, holding a duffle bag in his hand.

"What's crazy is, Stizz, you know how I get down for mines, and you go and do this. Nigga if you were fucked up, you could have hollered at me."

"Listen, Jordan. Just let us go, and you won't ever see us again," he tried begging.

"It's too late for that, my nigga," I said, putting a bullet through his temple. Mia was still holding her knee in pain crying when Ant put her out of her misery. "Come on, let's go."

~ ~ ~

After dropping everything off to Cash, I headed home because I knew Karma was going to be pissed at me. She had been blowing my phone up with text messages and calls. I realized that if I ever wanted to have a life with her, I needed to be done with this drug shit. I decided that no matter what, at the end of this month, it was over. I would convince Cash to let Trevor take over for me because they were family, and me and Karma would live happily ever after. If only life could have been that simple.

When I got home, I turned the key and opened the door, but the chain prevented me from gaining entrance. I could see Karma sitting on the couch, and it looked like she had been crying again.

"Karma, take the chain off the door, baby."

"For what? You fucked my sister, nigga, and you want me to let you in. You must be out of your fucking mind. Y'all can have each other."

"What are you talking about, Karma?" I asked. I should have known better than to do that with Rynesha. She probably snitched on me right after she left, because I didn't finish the job. I was fucked for real now. "Just open the door so we can talk, baby."

"No, let me die in peace!"

The word *die* made me kick the door in, snapping the chain. Karma sat in the dark with candles burning everywhere. In front of her, sitting on the coffee table, was a gun. I was easing my way over to grab it, but she snatched it up and aimed it at me.

"What the fuck is wrong with you?" I asked, stopping in my tracks. Looking into her eyes, I could tell that more was bothering her than just her finding out I fucked her sister. "Baby, put that gun down."

POP!

The bullet whizzed past my ear, missing me by inches. She began laughing incoherently, then fired the gun two more times. This time, one of the bullets hit me in the shoulder.

"Did you really think this was only about you fucking my sister? Niggas like you come and go, but family is forever," Karma said, holding up a phone. I just stared at her because I still didn't know what was going on. Sensing my puzzled look, she elaborated a little more to make me understand. "While you were gone, a phone started ringing. I thought you left your phone, but then I realized I had just finished talking to you an hour ago and you haven't been here since. I found the phone in your sweatpants, so I checked the messages."

"Karma, I can explain that," I said, knowing that she found my business phone. I had forgotten all about it when I changed my clothes.

"How can you explain killing my sister, Jordan? Huh? Tell me, you piece of shit."

"Baby, just please put the gun down and let me explain. I just need five minutes of your time."

"Talk!"

"I didn't know that was your sister. They tied us up and tried to rob us. We were just defending ourselves. I wish I could take back what happened, but I can't, baby. You have to believe me, I never meant to hurt you or your family."

I was trying to calm her down, at the same time easing my way closer to her in an effort to get that gun out of her hands. My shoulder was losing a lot of blood and needed medical attention, but I had to make sure she was okay first. She must have picked up on my sudden movements because she stepped back, aimed at my leg, and fired. Pain shot through me with such a force that it sent me falling to the floor.

"I told you not to move. The next move you make will cost you your life. I'm not playing."

The front door opened and her mom and Rynesha came in. I was relieved to see them because I thought Karma was really going to kill me. Her mom walked up to me, then without even thinking twice, spit in my face. It wasn't one of those regular spits either: she chugged up phlegm from deep within and let it rip. As it trickled down my face, I could see all the hatred she must have been feeling for me right now. It was written all over her face.

"How could you take my baby away from me like that?"

"I didn't know—"

Before I was able to get another word out, I felt a sharp kick to my side followed by another one. Rynesha was kicking me again and again with the heel of her shoe. They were torturing me. They say what's in the dark, soon comes to the light.

"What do you want to do with him?" Rynesha asked as I lay on the floor in pain.

Her mother's tears were now flowing freely from her eyes, and I knew where this was heading. If there was ever a time that I wished some nosey neighbor had called the police, this was one of them. I looked at Karma, and I knew she was the only chance I had of surviving this. I had to try to get through to her. My life was depending on it.

"Karma, please listen to me. You are not a killer. You're the same person that fell in love with me. I didn't mean to do that to your sister. If I would have known, I would have handled it differently. Please don't do this."

"Shut up! Shut your fucking mouth," Rynesha screamed.

"We can't do this here," Karma said, looking at the tremendous amount of blood that I had lost already, spreading across the floor. "Not in my house."

"Tie his ass up. We can take him somewhere else, then, because he's going to pay for what he did to my sister."

Their mother was the first to grab an extension cord from the drawer, then headed in my direction to tie my hands together. If they thought they were just going take me somewhere and kill me without me putting up a fight, they had another thing coming. Soon as she was close enough, I made my move. I gripped her arm and wrapped it behind her back, bringing it up to her neck so she couldn't move if she tried to. The pain from my shoulder and leg was excruciating, but I didn't let it stop me from fighting to get the hell out of there.

"Don't move, or I'll snap her arm out its socket," I said, holding her in the line of fire just in case Karma tried to get another shot off. At that moment, Rynesha had pulled out her own weapon. Shit was about to get ugly up in this bitch. My goal was, if I went, I was taking their mother with me. "Stay where you at, Rynesha. I'm dead serious."

"Let my fucking mother go," she said as they tried to surround me.

I used her as a shield and made my way toward the door. The only chance I had to get away was to make it outside and yell like a bitch, hoping that someone would come to the door and say they had called the police. The risk was high because if either of them were able to get off a good shot, I was a dead man. It was definitely a chance worth taking though. As soon as I had the door open, I pushed their mom in their direction and ran out yelling loudly.

"Somebody help me, please!"

Rynesha was the first one out the door ready to bust her gun, when I spotted their next-door neighbor's vehicle running. I don't know where the energy came from, but I suddenly got an adrenaline rush and ran to the car as fast as I could. By time Rynesha was able to get some shots off, I was speeding down the street.

"Damn, she really tried to down me," I said to myself, checking my rearview mirror, making sure I wasn't being followed. I had to hurry up and get out of this car before that lady reported it stolen. Hurt was all over my face as I headed to Cash's spot.

~ ~ ~

"Take it out, Cash! Take it out, it hurts!"

"Relax your muscles and stop tightening up, girl."

"No, it hurts. Put it back in my pussy, baby, come on."

"Aiight."

Not even the air conditioner that was set on high could stop Cash and his shorty from sweating their naked asses off. He pulled out of her ass and slid right back into her pussy, pumping away. He was hitting her with vicious strokes, as if he was trying to break her back. They were going at it so hard that they kept changing positions from doggy style to her riding him like an Indian girl on a horseback.

Cash squeezed her plump, round ass and stared at her flat stomach and small waist as she rode up and down on his dick. Her perky, handful-sized breasts bounced and jiggled wildly as she caressed her dark brown nipples while biting her full bottom lip. Her pussy was so wet and extremely warm, that her juices felt like soothing warm water running down his stomach as it secreted to his balls and thighs.

"Fuck me, Cash. Fuck me harder, baby!" she moaned out over the sounds of Miguel's smooth vocals, drowning out his voice momentarily. "That's it, daddy. That's my spot right there. This dick is so good! Tear this pussy up."

"This how you want it, huh?"

"Yeesssss! Fuck yeah," she moaned, sticking her fingers in her mouth.

Cash watched her rub her hands over her body, then over her tightly braided extensions that made her eyes look chinky. In all actuality, they were chinky, but her braids just added to the look. Brandi was very pretty. She was probably the prettiest girl on the north side, but also the freakiest. He was fucking her every which way possible, invading every hole in her body, except her nostrils and ears, when he heard loud banging on his front door.

"Yo, Cash. Open the door, nigga!" I yelled, trying to get his attention.

"Hold up, I'm coming!"

Cash was on the verge of busting all up in Brandi's good pussy, and here I was fucking up his groove. She didn't even bother getting off his dick because she was about to cum and wasn't going to let him or my knocking interrupt that. Cash watched as her eyes rolled to the back of her head as she dug her fingernails in his chest.

"Cash, don't stop. I'm about to cum. Oh shiiiittt, I'm cumming!"

Her body began to quake and quiver as she let out a deep invigorating sigh which caused Cash to tense up also. Before they knew it, they were both exploding together. After he released his semen inside her, he hopped out of the pussy and sat on the edge of the bed. The banging on the door got louder. He grabbed a towel and wrapped it around his waist. Brandi climbed underneath the sheets and sparked the half dutch that was lying on the nightstand. He headed downstairs to see why the fuck was I banging on his door like that. When he opened the door, I was lying on the steps. Blood was steadily seeping from my body.

"What the fuck! Jordan, what the hell happened to you?" Cash asked, helping me inside the house. By this time, I was so out of it that I didn't know where I was or how I made it there. "Who did this shit, Jay? Come on, bro, talk to me."

"They tried to kill me, but I was able to get away from them," I mumbled.

"Brandi, get down here, my brother got shot," Cash yelled, taking the towel off his body to try and stop the bleeding. He didn't care about the fact that he was standing there with his shit all out. All that mattered was making sure I didn't die. "Brandi, hurry the fuck up."

"I'm coming, damn," she said, running down the steps in a wifebeater and a pair of Cash's boxers. She immediately went to work trying to save me from bleeding to death.

Brandi was a nurse at a hospital, so she knew exactly what to do. Going to the hospital was out of the question for me with a gunshot wound, so she ran out to her car and came back with a medical bag. She set up an IV line, and once it was placed in my arm, she started operating to get the bullet that was still lodged in my shoulder out. The one in my leg went straight through. Cash stayed by my side the whole time Brandi was working.

"I'm calling my hitters and we're going to kill all of them," Cash said after I was stable and lying on the couch resting. "Tell me who did this, and they will be dead by the end of the day."

"Bro, it's not as simple as you think," I tried telling him, but he wasn't trying to hear none of it.

"Naw, fuck that shit, Jay. You lying up here all shot the fuck up, and you talking about this shit ain't that simple. Those drugs must've got your dumb ass on some delusional shit."

"Listen to me, Cash. Do you remember the bitch that me and Trevor popped at the hotel out in Jersey?" He nodded his head. "That was my girl's sister."

"What? Wait a minute! So you telling me that your girl popped you?" Cash smirked. "Damn, nigga, talk about tough love. I didn't know she had it in her."

"This shit ain't funny. I nearly made it out. Her mom and sister want me dead. Not to mention that she also found out that I fucked her other sister."

"So how you want to play this?" Cash asked, pouring us both a drink. Even though the shit was funny, he still wanted to kill her.

"Can we talk about it after I get some rest?" I said, feeling the effects of the drugs Brandi gave me.

"Get some rest bro! We'll be upstairs if you need anything," Cash said, heading back up to his room.

I lay on the couch, and within minutes I was sound asleep. When I woke up, it was so dark that I couldn't see anything. I reached over for the lamp and turned the light on. My life flashed before my eyes when I looked up and found three guns aimed at my face. Rynesha, Karma, and their mother were standing over me with smiles on their faces. I didn't know where Cash or Brandi was. I couldn't move or speak.

"What, you thought you were going to get away from us?" Karma said staring at me. "Nigga, you killed my sister and fucked my other sister. The penalty for that is death."

All three women started laughing uncontrollably. I closed my eyes and said a prayer. Before I could even beg for my life again, they all fired their weapons simultaneously into me.

POP! POP! POP!

BOOM! BOOM! BOOM!

BOCA! BOCA! BOCA!

I woke up in a cold sweat, feeling my body for holes, but finding none. My clothes were soaking wet from sweating. After adjusting my eyes, I realized that I was still in prison, in my cube, lying on my bunk. I couldn't believe that I was still locked up and everything that had happened to me was just a dream. I checked the time and date on my television realizing that I still had two days before I was released from prison. I went into the bathroom to change my clothes. As I stood there looking in the mirror, I thought about how I got to this point in my life. I shook my head smiling and said, "Karma's a bitch!"

TRAPPED IN LOVE 2 (THE SEQUEL)
COMING SOON!!

To order books, please fill out the order form below:
To order films please go to www.good2gofilms.com

Name:_____

Address:_____

City:_____State:_____Zip Code: _____

Phone:_____

Email:_____

Method of Payment: Check   VISA MASTERCARD

Credit Card#:__ _____

Name as it appears on card: _____

Signature: _____

Item Name	Price	Qty	Amount
48 Hours to Die – Silk White	$14.99		
A Hustler's Dream - Ernest Morris	$14.99		
A Hustler's Dream 2 - Ernest Morris	$14.99		
A Thug's Devotion – J. L. Rose and J. M. McMillon	$14.99		
All Eyes on Tommy Gunz – Warren Holloway	$14.99		
Black Reign – Ernest Morris	$14.99		
Bloody Mayhem Down South – Trayvon Jackson	$14.99		
Bloody Mayhem Down South 2 – Trayvon Jackson	$14.99		
Business Is Business – Silk White	$14.99		
Business Is Business 2 – Silk White	$14.99		
Business Is Business 3 – Silk White	$14.99		
Cash In Cash Out – Assa Raymond Baker	$14.99		
Cash In Cash Out 2 - Assa Raymond Baker	$14.99		
Childhood Sweethearts – Jacob Spears	$14.99		
Childhood Sweethearts 2 – Jacob Spears	$14.99		
Childhood Sweethearts 3 - Jacob Spears	$14.99		
Childhood Sweethearts 4 - Jacob Spears	$14.99		
Connected To The Plug – Dwan Marquis Williams	$14.99		
Connected To The Plug 2 – Dwan Marquis Williams	$14.99		
Connected To The Plug 3 – Dwan Williams	$14.99		
Cost of Betrayal – W.C. Holloway	$14.99		
Cost of Betrayal 2 – W.C. Holloway	$14.99		
Deadly Reunion – Ernest Morris	$14.99		
Dream's Life – Assa Raymond Baker	$14.99		
Flipping Numbers – Ernest Morris	$14.99		

Flipping Numbers 2 – Ernest Morris	$14.99		
He Loves Me, He Loves You Not - Mychea	$14.99		
He Loves Me, He Loves You Not 2 - Mychea	$14.99		
He Loves Me, He Loves You Not 3 - Mychea	$14.99		
He Loves Me, He Loves You Not 4 – Mychea	$14.99		
He Loves Me, He Loves You Not 5 – Mychea	$14.99		
Killing Signs – Ernest Morris	$14.99		
Kings of the Block – Dwan Willams	$14.99		
Kings of the Block 2 – Dwan Willams	$14.99		
Lord of My Land – Jay Morrison	$14.99		
Lost and Turned Out – Ernest Morris	$14.99		
Love & Dedication – W.C. Holloway	$14.99		
Love Hates Violence – De'Wayne Maris	$14.99		
Love Hates Violence 2 – De'Wayne Maris	$14.99		
Love Hates Violence 3 – De'Wayne Maris	$14.99		
Love Hates Violence 4 – De'Wayne Maris	$14.99		
Married To Da Streets – Silk White	$14.99		
M.E.R.C. - Make Every Rep Count Health and Fitness	$14.99		
Mercenary In Love – J.L. Rose & J.L. Turner	$14.99		
Money Make Me Cum – Ernest Morris	$14.99		
My Besties – Asia Hill	$14.99		
My Besties 2 – Asia Hill	$14.99		
My Besties 3 – Asia Hill	$14.99		
My Besties 4 – Asia Hill	$14.99		
My Boyfriend's Wife - Mychea	$14.99		
My Boyfriend's Wife 2 – Mychea	$14.99		
My Brothers Envy – J. L. Rose	$14.99		
My Brothers Envy 2 – J. L. Rose	$14.99		
Naughty Housewives – Ernest Morris	$14.99		
Naughty Housewives 2 – Ernest Morris	$14.99		
Naughty Housewives 3 – Ernest Morris	$14.99		
Naughty Housewives 4 – Ernest Morris	$14.99		
Never Be The Same – Silk White	$14.99		
Shades of Revenge – Assa Raymond Baker	$14.99		

Slumped – Jason Brent	$14.99		
Someone's Gonna Get It – Mychea	$14.99		
Stranded – Silk White	$14.99		
Supreme & Justice – Ernest Morris	$14.99		
Supreme & Justice 2 – Ernest Morris	$14.99		
Supreme & Justice 3 – Ernest Morris	$14.99		
Tears of a Hustler - Silk White	$14.99		
Tears of a Hustler 2 - Silk White	$14.99		
Tears of a Hustler 3 - Silk White	$14.99		
Tears of a Hustler 4- Silk White	$14.99		
Tears of a Hustler 5 – Silk White	$14.99		
Tears of a Hustler 6 – Silk White	$14.99		
The Last Love Letter – Warren Holloway	$14.99		
The Last Love Letter 2 – Warren Holloway	$14.99		
The Panty Ripper - Reality Way	$14.99		
The Panty Ripper 3 – Reality Way	$14.99		
The Solution – Jay Morrison	$14.99		
The Teflon Queen – Silk White	$14.99		
The Teflon Queen 2 – Silk White	$14.99		
The Teflon Queen 3 – Silk White	$14.99		
The Teflon Queen 4 – Silk White	$14.99		
The Teflon Queen 5 – Silk White	$14.99		
The Teflon Queen 6 - Silk White	$14.99		
The Vacation – Silk White	$14.99		
Tied To A Boss - J.L. Rose	$14.99		
Tied To A Boss 2 - J.L. Rose	$14.99		
Tied To A Boss 3 - J.L. Rose	$14.99		
Tied To A Boss 4 - J.L. Rose	$14.99		
Tied To A Boss 5 - J.L. Rose	$14.99		
Time Is Money - Silk White	$14.99		
Tomorrow's Not Promised – Robert Torres	$14.99		
Tomorrow's Not Promised 2 – Robert Torres	$14.99		
Two Mask One Heart – Jacob Spears and Trayvon Jackson	$14.99		
Two Mask One Heart 2 – Jacob Spears and Trayvon Jackson	$14.99		

Two Mask One Heart 3 – Jacob Spears and Trayvon Jackson	$14.99		
Wrong Place Wrong Time – Silk White	$14.99		
Young Goonz – Reality Way	$14.99		
Subtotal:			
Tax:			
Shipping (Free) U.S. Media Mail:			
Total:			

Make Checks Payable To: Good2Go Publishing, 7311 W Glass Lane, Laveen, AZ 85339

CPSIA information can be obtained
at www.ICGtesting.com
Printed in the USA
LVHW041600100320
649602LV00009B/844

9 781947 340503